OWL IN THE OFFICE

'This could be the last creature I'm able to help, I'm afraid, Mandy. The buildings are badly in need of repair and it's going to cost at least five hundred pounds to have them done.'

'Five hundred pounds!' Mandy gasped.

'Yes,' Betty said, shaking her head. 'And to cap it all, Sam Western's put up my rent. I simply don't have enough money to pay him, do the repairs *and* feed the animals as well.'

'But you *can't* close down, Betty,' Mandy said, almost in tears. 'You just can't! What will happen to all the animals you've got here?'

'I'll find homes for as many as possible,' Betty said. 'But I'm afraid the rest will have to be destroyed . . .'

Animal Ark series

1 Kittens in the Kitchen
2 Pony in the Porch
3 Puppies in the Pantry
4 Goat in the Garden
5 Hedgehogs in the Hall
6 Badger in the Basement
7 Cub in the Cupboard
8 Piglet in a Playpen
9 Owl in the Office
10 Lamb in the Laundry
11 Bunnies in the Bathroom
12 Donkey on the Doorstep
13 Hamster in a Hamper
14 Goose on the Loose
15 Calf in the Cottage
16 Koalas in a Crisis
17 Wombat in the Wild
18 Roo on the Rock
19 Squirrels in the School
20 Guinea-pig in the Garage
21 Fawn in the Forest
22 Shetland in the Shed
23 Swan in the Swim
24 Lion by the Lake
25 Elephants in the East
26 Monkeys on the Mountain
27 Dog at the Door
28 Foals in the Field
29 Sheep at the Show
30 Racoons on the Roof
31 Dolphin in the Deep
32 Bears in the Barn
33 Otter in the Outhouse
34 Whale in the Waves
35 Hound at the Hospital
36 Rabbits on the Run
37 Horse in the House
38 Panda in the Park
39 Tiger on the Track
40 Gorilla in the Glade
41 Tabby in the Tub
42 Chinchilla up the Chimney
43 Puppy in a Puddle
44 Leopard at the Lodge
45 Giraffe in a Jam
46 Hippo in a Hole
47 Foxes on the Farm
48 Badgers by the Bridge
49 Deer on the Drive
50 Animals in the Ark
51 Mare in the Meadow
52 Cats in the Caravan
Hauntings 1: Dog in the Dungeon
Hauntings 2: Cat in the Crypt
Hauntings 3: Stallion in the Storm
Hauntings 4: Wolf at the Window
Hauntings 5: Hound on the Heath
Hauntings 6: Colt in the Cave
Ponies at the Point
Seal on the Shore
Pigs at the Picnic
Sheepdog in the Snow
Kitten in the Cold
Fox in the Frost
Hamster in the Holly
Pony in the Post
Pup at the Palace
Mouse in the Mistletoe
Animal Ark Favourites
Wildlife Ways

LUCY DANIELS

Owl — in the — Office

Illustrations by Shelagh McNicholas

a division of Hodder Headline Limited

To Rats and Jess and their cousins,
Midge and Milo.

Special thanks to Sue Welford for all her help. Thanks also to C. J. Hall, B.Vet.Med., M.R.C.V.S., for reviewing the veterinary information contained in this book and to Tom Tyrell of the Tomar Owl Sanctuary.

Created by Working Partners Limited, London W6 0QT
Original series created by Ben M. Baglio

First published in Great Britain in 1995
by Hodder Children's Books
This edition published in 2001

For more information on Animal Ark, please contact:
www.animalark.co.uk

20

A catalogue record for this book is available from the British Library

ISBN 0 340 61931 7

Typeset by Avon Dataset Ltd, Bidford-on-Avon B50 4JH
Printed and bound in Great Britain by
Clays Ltd, St Ives plc

Hodder Children's Books
a division of Hodder Headline Limited
338 Euston Road
London NW1 3BH

One

'Quick, James – over here!' Mandy Hope shouted to her friend, James Hunter. She knelt down in a pile of last autumn's fallen leaves, gently brushing some aside.

Mandy and James were out walking in Monkton Spinney near Welford, the Yorkshire village where they lived. Mandy had spotted something in the carpet of leaves beneath one of the oak trees.

'What have you found?' James ran over and skidded to a halt beside her. His trainers sent up a spray of leaves. He pushed his glasses back up his nose and looked down at the little hollow Mandy had made in the leaves.

Mandy cupped her hands together and lifted something very carefully from the ground. She held what looked like a bundle of bedraggled feathers. Two round, dark eyes stared at James. A sharp, hooked beak opened and a kind of creaky noise came out. It sounded like a gate that needed oiling. Mandy drew in her breath. She gazed up at James with shining eyes.

'Oh! Look, it's a baby owl.'

James touched the tiny creature gently with his fingertip. 'What kind of owl is it?'

'A tawny owl, I think,' said Mandy. 'Oh, the poor thing!' She had thought it might be an owl when she first spied the bundle of grey-brown flecked feathers lying in its hollow of leaves. Although she'd seen pictures of baby owls she had never actually seen a live one. It felt soft and beautiful and very fragile.

'Wow!' exclaimed James. His eyes were round behind his spectacles. 'Where did it come from, Mandy?'

Mandy looked up into the huge oak tree, its great branches reaching up to the sky.

'Up there somewhere,' she said, frowning. 'You can never really see owl's nests; they're too well hidden. It's probably where two of those big branches meet or maybe in an old squirrel's drey somewhere.'

Mandy's heart jolted with pity. 'Poor thing,' she murmured again.

James squinted upwards, pushing back the peak of his baseball cap to get a better view. 'Maybe we could climb up and put it back in its nest,' he suggested hopefully.

Mandy knew it would be the best solution. The owl wouldn't survive for long out in the open, that was for sure. But how on earth were they to reach it?

'We'd need a ladder.' Mandy tucked a strand of blonde hair behind her ear. Her brows knitted together over her blue eyes in a thoughtful frown. 'Or maybe I could climb up?' she said, not sounding at all sure. She had long legs and was pretty good at climbing trees but this one had a tall, straight trunk with no footholds at all.

'No way,' said James with a shake of his head. 'The first branch is miles up. Don't you think we should just leave it where it is?'

Mandy stared at him in horror. 'We can't do that! It'll get eaten by a fox or something!'

James shrugged. 'I read somewhere you should

leave baby birds alone. Sometimes their parents come down to feed them.'

Mandy shook her head. 'Owls mostly come out at night,' she said. 'It could be too late by the time they find him.' She heaved a sigh. There was only one thing to do then. They would have to take the baby owl back to Animal Ark. Her mum and dad were both veterinary surgeons. They would know what to do.

'We'll have to take it back with us.' she said to James.

James bit his lip. Once Mandy made up her mind about something, there was no changing it.

James whistled to his dog. Blackie crashed through the undergrowth towards them.

'Come on, Blackie.' James patted the Labrador's sleek head. 'Time to go home.'

But Blackie was too interested in Mandy's mysterious bundle to take any notice of his master. He jumped up, sniffing the owl's feathers.

'Down,' Mandy commanded. Blackie ignored her and went on sniffing.

James pulled his collar gently. 'Blackie, do as you're told!'

Blackie wasn't the most obedient dog, but this time he listened to James and allowed himself to be pulled away from the baby owl.

Mandy carefully wrapped the owlet in her scarf and cradled it gently in her arms. 'Come on then, James. The sooner we get this little thing into the warm, the better.'

Blackie soon lost interest and trotted on ahead.

'What do you feed owls on?' James trudged along by Mandy's side as they made their way through the spinney, out towards the road that led to the village of Welford.

Mr and Mrs Hope ran a busy veterinary practice in the village. They had adopted Mandy when she was a baby. Her natural parents had been killed in a car crash and Mandy couldn't remember anything about them. The Hopes were the only parents Mandy had ever known. As far as she was concerned nobody could wish for a better mother or father.

James, a year younger, was Mandy's best friend. He shared her love of animals. Mandy and James both went to school in the neighbouring town of Walton. Today though, was the first day of the spring half-term.

'I'm not sure,' Mandy said in answer to James's question. She knew that in the wild, owls hunted for small mammals like mice and voles. Owls hunted mostly at night, although sometimes you saw them out in the daytime, especially during springtime when they had young to feed. But Mandy couldn't exactly imagine catching little furry animals to feed the baby owl. In fact Mandy wasn't sure *what* she was going to do with it. All she knew was that they couldn't leave the tiny, helpless creature out in the woods with no one to protect it.

The bird peeped out with huge, scared eyes as they made their way across the village green towards the old stone cottage with its wooden sign that said 'Animal Ark, Veterinary Surgeon'. Mr and Mrs Hope had started the practice when they got married. Mr Hope had lived in Welford all his life and both he and his wife were well known and popular members of the village community.

Mandy and James hurried in through the surgery door. Jean Knox, the receptionist, was busy at her computer. She looked up as Mandy and James burst in.

'Where's Mum and Dad?' Mandy asked breathlessly, cradling the owlet against her coat.

Jean glanced at the diary in front of her. 'Your dad's gone up to Syke Farm and your mum's indoors.' She peered over the top of her glasses.

'What *have* you got there, Mandy?'

Mandy went closer and gently peeled back the woolly scarf.

Jean's hand flew to her mouth. 'Oh, my goodness. Where did you get that?'

Mandy explained quickly.

'We couldn't possibly reach the owl's nest,' James blurted. 'So we had to bring it here.'

'Well, whatever next. Take it out to Simon. He'll know what to do for the best,' Jean said matter-of-factly. It was no real surprise to her when Mandy arrived home with a sick or abandoned animal. If Mandy had arrived home with a baby elephant, Jean probably wouldn't have batted an eyelid. Mandy loved all animals and wanted to be a vet herself one day.

Simon, the veterinary nurse, was sterilising the surgical instruments. It had been a busy morning: a cat with a thorn in its paw; a dog that had swallowed a sock; five puppies for injections; a rabbit with pneumonia and a gerbil whose babies were ready to be born. Then to cap it all, fussy Mrs Ponsonby from Bleakfell Hall had arrived with Pandora, her pampered Pekinese, just as they were closing. It had taken all of Mrs Hope's powers of persuasion to convince Mrs Ponsonby that her dog didn't have flu, just a runny nose.

Simon looked up and grinned when Mandy and James walked in.

'Hello, you two,' he said cheerily. 'What have you been up to this morning?'

'We found this . . .' Mandy pulled back the scarf to reveal the baby owl.

'Oh, wow!' Simon touched the creature's head. 'Where?'

James explained.

Simon frowned and ran his hand over his fair hair. 'You know, you should really have left him there.'

'I *told* you!' James said.

Mandy began to wonder if she had done the right thing in bringing the owl to the surgery. But it was too late now. Rightly or wrongly she had brought him home and it was now her responsibility to look after him. 'But I couldn't just leave him,' she protested.

Simon pulled a wry face. 'I know it's hard, Mandy, but the parents may have come down to feed him – or he might have been able to find his way back to the nest.'

Mandy shook her head firmly. 'No, I'm sure he's too weak for that.'

Simon looked at the tiny creature. 'Well, maybe

you're right. If he's the smallest chick the others probably hogged all the food and he probably would have starved to death anyway.'

Simon pulled back the scarf a little more. 'He's very tiny. I'm afraid it's the survival of the fittest where birds in the nest are concerned. Nature can be very cruel at times.'

'It certainly can,' Mandy said. The little owl looked so sweet. To never have known if it lived or died would have been too much to bear.

'I think the best thing to do . . .' Simon suggested, 'is to take the little fellow up to the animal sanctuary. I'm sure Betty Hilder will know what's best.'

Just then, Emily Hope came through the door. She was still wearing her white vet's coat, and her red hair was tied up with a green silk scarf. She smiled. 'Hi, you two.' Then she spied the small bundle in the crook of Mandy's arm. 'What have you brought us now, Mandy?'

Mandy quickly explained.

'Simon says we should have left him there,' said James.

Mrs Hope raised her eyebrows. 'Yes, you should have done really. But now he *is* here, let's take a look at him.'

'Simon suggested we take him up to Betty,' said Mandy.

Mrs Hope agreed. 'Good idea,' she said. 'I'll take a look at him first though. He could be injured. Was he just lying on the ground?'

'Well, he was *sitting* on the ground,' Mandy said. 'In fact,' she added, 'I almost trod on him.'

'OK,' Mrs Hope said in her usual businesslike manner. She took a pair of surgical gloves out of their sealed polythene packet and pulled them on. 'Sit up on the couch, Mandy and I'll take a look at him.'

Mandy heaved herself up. She gently unwrapped the little owl and set him carefully on her knee. Free of the woolly scarf, he shook his feathers, staggered and almost fell. His sharp claws gripped the knee of Mandy's jeans as he struggled to regain his balance.

Mandy put her hands either side to steady him, smoothing down the soft feathers. She was surprised to feel how tiny his body was. The owl sat there blinking in the bright overhead light. Then, without warning, he flapped his wings and tried to fly, overbalancing completely and landing in a heap on the scrubbed tiles of the surgery floor.

Mandy jumped down and bent to retrieve him,

worried in case the owl had landed awkwardly. It would be too bad if the little bird had survived its fall from the nest then ended up hurting itself on the surgery floor!

'Mind those talons,' her mother warned. 'You might get a nasty scratch.'

Mandy put her hands either side of the bird's wings. 'Now, behave yourself, Mr Owl,' she said sternly. The owl blinked at her and made a squeak. Mandy couldn't help smiling. He looked rather indignant at being handled by a human being! She set him down on her knee again. This time, he stayed where he was.

Mrs Hope quickly examined the bird. Feet, wings, fluffy head. Finally she smoothed down its feathers. 'He's very thin,' she said, frowning. 'Skin and bone. I reckon he hasn't been getting much food. Just wrap him up again, Mandy. I'll take a look at his eyes and beak.'

'Mum, can't I keep him here?' Mandy said. 'I'll look after him, I promise. I'll get food for him and everything.'

Mrs Hope shook her head. 'Sorry, Mandy. Looking after baby owls is really very specialised. Simon's right, we'd better take it to the sanctuary. Betty will know what's best.'

Mandy knew better than to argue with her mother. A veterinary surgery was no place to keep a baby owl. However much Mandy longed to take care of it, she knew expert help was needed.

Mrs Hope looked at her watch. 'I could take you up there now if you like. I haven't got any calls to make until a bit later.'

'That would be great, Mum. Thanks.' Mandy got down off the couch. 'Coming, James?'

'You bet!'

'You'd better put Blackie in the back,' Mrs Hope told James when they got outside. Blackie was still trying to find out what Mandy had in her arms, jumping up and sniffing at the scarf. 'He seems a bit too nosy if you ask me.'

Blackie was always curious about everything. And his curiosity often got him into trouble.

James opened the rear door of the four-wheel drive and banged his hand on the floor. Blackie jumped inside.

'Stay!' James commanded.

For once, Blackie did as he was told. He sat looking out of the window, his tail wagging like mad. Every trip in a car was an adventure to him.

They all piled in and Mrs Hope set off through the village. She turned off past the post office, heading for the narrow hill road that led up to the Welford Animal Sanctuary.

'Mum,' Mandy said when they were halfway there. She had been feeling a bit upset about taking the owl away from its natural environment. 'I'm sorry if I've done the wrong thing.'

Mrs Hope patted her knee. 'It just might be better to ask someone's advice next time, that's all.'

'I will,' Mandy promised. She made a vow to listen to James a bit more too. She couldn't *always* be right.

Mandy had been to the sanctuary several times

before and knew its owner, Betty Hilder, very well. Although she loved seeing the animals Betty had rescued, her heart always went out to them. She knew that most of them would have had to be put to sleep if Betty hadn't taken them in. There were creatures of every kind. Dogs, cats, donkeys, a Shetland pony, an ancient goat with three legs. The last time Mandy had been there, Betty even had a Vietnamese pot-bellied pig that someone had brought in.

'They had bought it as a pet,' Betty had explained to Mandy. 'No one ever told them that pigs are extremely difficult to house-train.'

The car crested the summit of the hill and began the winding descent down the other side.

Mandy gazed out of the car window at the panorama of hills and dales. The dry-stone walls made a picturesque pattern across the landscape. The sky was blue and broad, not a cloud to be seen.

Mandy loved it up here on the moor, the village of Welford spread out below. There were the two roads, the church and the village green in the middle. A pall of smoke rose from the row of quaint old cottages behind the Fox and Goose pub. Her grandad's friend, Walter Pickard, lived in one.

They'd both been bell-ringers at the church for years. Mr Pickard must be having a bonfire, burning his garden rubbish probably. The village people took great pride in their gardens and Walter grew roses that won prizes at the Welford Show every year.

Mrs Hope changed gear and swung the four-wheel drive round into the drive that led up to the sanctuary. To Mandy's dismay, the gate was shut and locked.

'Oh!' she exclaimed, puzzled. 'I've never seen it shut before.'

Mandy wondered what on earth had happened. Betty was always proud to be able to say the sanctuary was open any time.

Mrs Hope pulled up in front of the gate. 'Maybe she's gone out shopping,' she suggested. 'I'll just get out and see.'

Mrs Hope went up to the gate. She stood frowning at the rows of kennels and outbuildings that housed the rescued animals. Then, Betty Hilder, a young woman dressed in baggy jeans and a thick jumper, came out of her bungalow and hurried to open the gate. She spoke to Mrs Hope.

'I wonder what they're talking about,' said James.

'I don't know,' said Mandy, still worried. 'Betty looks a bit upset.'

Betty took out a key and unlocked the gate. Mrs Hope came back to the car looking grim. As soon as she opened the door they bombarded her with questions.

'What's up, Mum?' asked Mandy, her heart pounding. She had a feeling something really serious was going on.

'Why is Betty looking so upset?' asked James.

Mrs Hope turned on the ignition. 'I'm afraid it's bad news, you two,' she said. 'Betty's letting *us* in but she's had to close the sanctuary to the general public.'

Mandy leaned forward anxiously. 'Closed! Mum . . . why?'

Mrs Hope drove through the gate and into the concrete yard. A chorus of dogs greeted the newcomers as they got out of the car. In the back, Blackie barked excitedly and clawed at the window.

'Quiet, Blackie!' James commanded.

'Betty's very short of money,' Mrs Hope told Mandy and James as she shut the car door. 'She just can't afford to keep things going.'

'What will happen to the animals?' said Mandy. She glanced down at the tiny, helpless bundle in her arms. If Betty wasn't going to be able to look after the baby owl then who would? There wasn't another sanctuary for miles.

Her mother glanced at her. 'If they can't be found homes, then–' She broke off. Mandy had a horrible sinking feeling she knew exactly what her mum was going to say. If the animals couldn't be found homes then they would all have to be destroyed!

'No!' Mandy turned to James. 'We can't let the animals be put to sleep,' she cried. 'We've got to do something. We've just *got* to!'

Two

As Mandy went towards the bungalow clutching her precious bundle, Betty pulled back the scarf and took a peek at the owl.

'Poor thing,' she said. 'Bring it into the office, Mandy. It's warmer in there.'

They went into the room where Betty kept her old typewriter and telephone. There were papers all over the desk, photos of cats and dogs on the wall and a bucket of pony nuts in one corner.

Two cats came over and rubbed themselves against Mandy's legs. Betty shooed them out. She went through another door and brought back a large cage with a wooden back. 'We'll put him in this hospital cage for the time being,' she said. 'He's got to be isolated in case he's carrying any pests or diseases.'

Mandy handed over her precious bundle. Betty quickly examined the bird.

'I've already taken a look at it,' Mrs Hope confirmed. 'It's uninjured but very thin. I think it must have been the smallest of the brood.'

Betty went over to the cupboard and took out a plastic bottle. She covered the owl's face with one hand then quickly puffed a white powder into its feathers.

'That's to get rid of any vermin,' she explained.

Betty placed the owlet carefully in the cage. A cloud of white dust flew out as it shook its feathers then settled in one corner looking hunched up and miserable.

Betty perched on the edge of the desk. She looked thoughtful. 'I've had a couple of owls before,' she said. 'They both went over to Longmoor Owl Rehabilitation Centre. Once I've persuaded this one to eat properly I'll take it over there. They'll keep it for a few weeks then release it back into the wild as soon as it's fit.'

'Couldn't we do that?' asked Mandy. She felt

disappointed. She would love to have seen the owl fly safely away.

Betty shook her head. 'I'm not licensed to do that,' she explained. 'And the owl must never be handled again once it's accepting food, otherwise it'll never be able to be released. I haven't got those kind of facilities here, Mandy.'

'Why mustn't you handle it?' asked James.

'Because it will learn to rely on humans to feed it,' explained Betty.

'What will you give it?' James asked. He peered into the cage. The owl blinked slowly at him.

'Well,' Betty said thoughtfully. 'I'll have to force-feed it at first. Owls mainly eat small mammals and birds in the woodlands. In the summer they hunt more in the open and catch rabbits, moles – even earthworms.'

'I could go and dig up some worms,' said James.

'I shouldn't worry just yet, James,' Betty said. 'He won't eat anything for a while. And he couldn't have worms for long. Owls need feathers and bones in their diet. I'll try and get some chicks from the chicken farm if they'll give them to me.' She glanced at Mrs Hope. 'This could be the last creature I'm able to help, I'm afraid, Mandy. The buildings are badly in need of repair and it's going to cost at least five hundred pounds to have them done.'

'Five hundred pounds!' Mandy gasped.

'Yes,' Betty said, shaking her head. 'And to cap it all, Sam Western's put up my rent. I simply don't have enough money to pay him, do the repairs *and* feed the animals as well.'

Sam Western was a local farmer who ran his large farm like a factory. He was well-known for being both bad-tempered and mean. He was a tough businessman with no love for animals. He wouldn't care what happened to the waifs and strays at the sanctuary if it had to close.

Mandy's sadness turned to anger. 'Why has Mr Western done a mean thing like that?' she blurted.

'I think he wants the bungalow for one of his farm workers,' Betty explained. 'He knows I can't afford to pay him a higher rent.'

'But you *can't* close down, Betty,' Mandy said, almost in tears. 'The sanctuary is your life!'

'I'm sorry, Mandy,' Betty said, sounding close to tears herself. 'I really don't have any choice.'

'But what will happen to all the animals you've got here?' cried Mandy.

'I'll find homes for as many as possible,' Betty

said. 'I've been in touch with the RSPCA but they've told me they're overcrowded already. I'm afraid the rest will have to be destroyed.'

It was just as Mandy had feared. 'James and I are going to try to think of a way to get some money to help you,' she said.

'That's right,' James agreed, nodding his head like mad.

Betty sighed. 'I'm very grateful, you two, but I'm afraid it'll take more than your pocket money to save this place.'

'Oh, no,' said Mandy. 'I mean *raise* money like we do at school. We need to sit down and make a plan. Isn't that right, James?'

'Yup,' James nodded fiercely. 'We're going to do it as soon as we get back home.'

'That's very kind of you,' Betty said gratefully. 'But five hundred pounds is an awful lot of money, I'm afraid.'

'I'll give you my pocket money to help pay for the owl's food,' Mandy glanced at her mother with shining eyes. 'That'll be OK, won't it, Mum?'

Mrs Hope patted her daughter's shoulder. 'Yes, of course, Mandy, every little helps.'

'So you'll be able to keep the baby owl here for now?' Mandy asked Betty.

Betty nodded. 'Yes, I promise. I'll ring the chicken farm straight away. Perhaps you'd like to come back in a couple of days, Mandy, to see how he's getting on?'

'You bet,' said Mandy. 'I wouldn't miss it for the world. Please try to hang on, Betty. We'll think of something; I know we will!'

Mandy and James left Mrs Hope talking to Betty and wandered outside

In the paddock, Bubbles, a fat, black Shetland pony with short legs trotted up to the fence when he saw Mandy and James. Bubbles had been

rescued by Betty when his owner's children had outgrown him. He put his nose through the rails and nuzzled Mandy's sleeve. With tears in her eyes, she fondled his coarse forelock.

'I can't bear to think of it, James,' she sniffed. 'Poor old Bubbles might have to be put down.'

'I know,' James said glumly. 'No one's going to want an old pony like him. That's why he's here in the first place.'

'*I* would,' Mandy said indignantly. 'I'd love to have him.' But in her heart she knew it was impossible. There was no room at Animal Ark to keep a pony, even one as small as Bubbles.

They left Bubbles and walked between the lines of dog kennels. Some were badly in need of repair. In one, a small mongrel jumped up at the wire when it saw them coming. The dog's name, Midge, was written on a plaque by the door.

'Hello, Midge.' Mandy knelt to stroke the puppy. It wagged its tail, jumping up to try to lick her face through the wire.

Mandy stood up with a sigh. The dog whined pitifully as they walked away.

'Look,' said Mandy. 'There's old Clarence, that ram Betty saved from slaughter. And that Jersey heifer Sam Western was going to have killed because she's only got one eye.'

'No one's going to want her, either,' James said sadly. He stood on the bottom rail of the fence and scratched the heifer's poll.

'Come on,' Mandy said with another sigh. 'Let's go and sit in the car and try to think what we can do to help.'

Mrs Hope came out of the office with Betty. 'Thanks, Betty,' she said. 'We'll come up again as soon as we can.'

Mandy and James said their goodbyes and climbed into the car. Blackie greeted them with a wildly wagging tail.

Mandy patted his head absent-mindedly. There was no time to waste. If they didn't think of something to save the sanctuary *soon,* it could well be too late!

'Why don't we just go and see Mr Western?' Mandy suggested as they drove out of the gate. She turned to wave to Betty as she closed and locked the gate behind them. 'We could just ask him not to put the rent up.'

Mrs Hope shook her head. 'Don't be daft, Mandy. You know what type of man he is. He's a businessman as well as a farmer. He won't care about stray animals. They're not worth twopence to someone like him.'

Mandy sighed. 'It might be worth a *try*.'

'No, Mandy,' Mrs Hope said firmly. 'I can promise you it wouldn't.'

On the way back to Animal Ark, Mandy and James tried to come up with a way to raise money.

'We could have a jumble sale,' James suggested.

'Where would you hold it?' Mrs Hope asked.

'The village hall?' said James.

Mrs Hope glanced at them in the mirror. 'It's usually booked up ages in advance. I'm afraid Betty needs that money pretty urgently.'

Mandy pulled a thoughtful face. 'How about a sponsored swim at school, then?' she said. Then her face fell. Swimming in the school's outdoor pool at this time of year wouldn't be any fun at all. Nobody was *that* silly. No, they had to think of something else.

'A sponsored bike ride?' James piped up. 'Loads of people would do it. Your grandad for instance.'

Mandy bit her lip. 'That's not a bad idea, James. But we had one last term, remember? People might not want to do one again so quickly.'

'That's true,' James said, raising his eyebrows.

All the way home, Mandy racked her brains.

Most of her friends in the village were animal lovers. And most owned pets of one kind or another. She felt sure they would want to help. But it had to be more than just *giving* money. There were so many charities needing funds. The Reverend Hadcroft had started an appeal to repair the church roof. There was a big board by the lichgate with marks to show how much money had been raised. The marker was only up to two hundred pounds so he needed lots more before work on the roof could even begin.

Someone from the village was always calling round collecting money for charities – guide dogs for the blind, the lifeboat men. They were all very good causes. If Mandy and James were going to get money for the sanctuary it had to be something the villagers could really get involved in – something that would be fun *and* raise funds at the same time. Something that had never happened in Welford before.

As Mrs Hope drove along the village high street with its pretty green in the centre and old-fashioned shops, Mandy suddenly brightened.

'I know,' she said. 'Let's go and see Gran and Grandad. They'll help us think of something.'

'Good idea,' said James. 'Maybe your gran's

done some baking. All this thinking is making me hungry!'

Mandy's grandparents lived just up the road from Animal Ark, in a house called Lilac Cottage.

In the drive, Mandy's grandad was unloading plastic carrier bags from his new camper van. He looked delighted to see them.

'Come in and have a cup of tea!' he called.

Mrs Hope wound down her window. 'I'd love to, Dad,' she called to her father-in-law. 'But I've got a few calls to make. These two want to pick your brains.'

Grandad ran his hand through his thatch of white hair. 'What now?' he asked with a broad grin.

Mandy and James jumped out of the back. James opened the rear door for Blackie. Blackie ran up to Grandad and stuck his nose into one of the carrier bags.

'Blackie!' James shouted. He ran to grab the dog's collar.

'The animal sanctuary's going to have to close and we're trying to think of a way to save it – oh, Grandad, you've got to help us!' Mandy said all in one breath.

Grandad put his arm round her shoulders. 'Now

calm down, Mandy. Help me with these bags and we'll go and see what Gran can find us to eat. No good thinking on an empty stomach.' He waved to Mrs Hope. 'See you later, Emily.'

Mrs Hope put the car into gear and drove off down the street.

By now, Blackie had pulled out a packet of crisps. It was clamped firmly between his teeth and he was shaking it to and fro, growling. James was desperately trying to get it away from him.

'I'm ever so sorry, Mr Hope.' James went red. Trust Blackie to show him up.

'Oh, let him have it,' Mandy's grandfather said amiably. 'It can be his elevenses.'

James let go the other end of the crisp packet and it suddenly burst all over the path. Blackie ran around gobbling up crisps like a vacuum cleaner.

Laughing, Mandy and James helped Mr Hope carry the shopping indoors. They went up the garden path, under the budding lilac tree that gave the cottage its name, and in through the back door.

In the cosy kitchen, with its pine cupboards and bright red gingham curtains, Mandy's grandmother was putting groceries away in the larder.

The kettle was already boiling on the worktop by the sink.

'Mandy, James, where did you come from?' Gran exclaimed as they all came into the kitchen. She looked delighted to see them.

Mandy put the carrier bags on the kitchen table and ran to give her grandmother a hug. She loved coming to the cottage and chatting with her grandparents. Whenever she had a problem, they always seemed to find the answers.

'What's up, Mandy?' Gran said, looking at her knowingly. She always seemed to sense when something was wrong.

Grandad came in. 'She's getting in a stew over the animal sanctuary,' he said.

Over steaming mugs of hot chocolate and a plate of home-made cookies, Mandy and James told them the full story.

'So you see,' Mandy said unhappily, 'we've got to get a move on. And at the moment we just can't think of *anything*. Can we, James?'

James shook his head, his mouth too full to speak.

Gran and Grandad looked glum.

'It's going to take a great deal of money to ensure the sanctuary stays open, Mandy,' Grandad said doubtfully. 'Those places are expensive to run.'

'I know, Grandad,' Mandy said, her eyes bright. 'Betty needs five hundred pounds to repair the buildings right away. That's why we've got to think of something really original, something everyone will want to help with.'

'I suggested a sponsored bike ride,' said James.

'Great idea!' said Mandy's grandfather. He was an enthusiastic bike rider and could often be seen pedalling in the countryside surrounding the village.

'But we had one last term,' James went on. 'Mandy said people won't want to do that again.'

'That's probably true,' said Grandad, looking serious again. He looked at his wife expectantly. 'Come on, Dorothy. You're usually full of ideas.'

Mandy's grandmother was always campaigning for something or other; writing letters to Parliament, getting up petitions. Not long ago she'd saved the village post office from being closed down. This time though, she seemed stumped.

Gran took off her glasses and laid them on the table. She rubbed her eyes. 'I know,' she said suddenly. 'How about a sponsored dog walk?'

'That's a good idea,' said James. 'Blackie would love that.'

At the word 'walk' Blackie's ears pricked up. He jumped up and put his front paws on the table. His tongue lolled out and his tail was wagging furiously.

'No, Blackie,' James said patiently. 'We're not going for a walk. Not now.' He tried to push Blackie down but the dog refused to budge. He just barked and wagged his tail harder still.

Mandy laughed. 'You'll have to stop saying that word, James.'

'Down, Blackie!' James frowned, sneaking Blackie a piece of biscuit to make sure he did as he was told.

'It's a good idea, Gran,' Mandy went on. 'But a dog would only involve people who own dogs.'

'How about a *pet* walk?' said Gran putting her glasses back on. She said the word 'walk' quietly so Blackie wouldn't hear.

Mandy giggled in spite of herself. 'Oh, Gran. I can't see anyone wanting to sponsor a tortoise! I want to get the whole village involved.'

'Well . . .' Grandad said slowly, 'how about one of those shows? You know, where you get a prize for the best rabbit, the most obedient dog – that sort of thing.' He brushed a crumb from his moustache. 'Then even people with pet spiders will be able to take part.' He sat back looking pleased with himself.

Mandy took a deep breath. What a terrific idea! Trust Grandad to come up trumps.

She jumped up from her chair and ran to give her grandfather a hug. 'Oh, Grandad, that's brilliant! We could have the best cat, the best hamster . . . even the best *rat*. We could call it the Grand Novelty Village Pet Show.'

'Well,' said her grandmother. 'That does sound *very* grand indeed.'

'It will be,' Mandy said. 'It will be the grandest event the village had ever seen. Oh, Grandad, it's perfect!'

'I've got an idea,' James said. He had been looking very thoughtful.

They all gazed at him expectantly.

'What?' asked Mandy.

'We could call our campaign SOS.'

'SOS?' asked Grandad, looking puzzled.

'Yup,' said James smugly. 'Save Our Sanctuary.'

Mandy took one last gulp of hot chocolate and slammed her mug down on the table. She ran the back of her hand across her mouth. 'Come on,

James. Let's get back to Animal Ark. I'll phone Betty to see if she thinks it's a good idea too. Then we'll start making plans!'

Three

James hurriedly finished his biscuit. He said goodbye to Mandy's grandparents and dashed after Mandy. She was already halfway down the road.

'Come *on*, James,' she called over her shoulder. 'There's no time to waste!'

When they arrived at Animal Ark, a woman dressed in old black wellington boots and a brown jacket stood on the path outside the surgery door. She was desperately hanging on to the halter of a restless black goat. The goat had perky ears and a tail that waggled about as if it were on a spring. The woman was obviously having trouble holding him. The goat's delicate hooves clattered on the path like castanets.

It was Lydia Fawcett from High Cross Farm. She owned a herd of lively goats and this one looked as if it was the liveliest of them all! But Lydia usually treated her animals with home-made remedies. She never came to the vets' unless something was seriously wrong. What on earth was she doing here?

Mandy ran up to her. 'Hello, Lydia. Can I help?' she asked, almost laughing at the goat's antics. He certainly didn't look very sick.

Lydia twisted the halter in an effort to steady him. 'Oh, yes, please, Mandy,' she said. 'Could you go in and get your father for me? Monty's got a really bad leg. I've tried to treat it myself but it's getting worse.'

Mandy stared at the goat. It was leaping about on three legs like a ballet dancer. James stood at the gate, his hand over his mouth to try to stop himself laughing. He held tightly on to Blackie's lead. If Monty broke free, there was nothing Blackie liked better than a good game of chase.

'Hang on,' Mandy said, 'I'll go and fetch someone.' She ran in through the surgery door.

Mr Hope was writing up his notes from morning

surgery. He looked up and gave a broad, lop-sided grin as Mandy rushed in. 'What's up?'

'Dad,' Mandy said urgently, 'Lydia's outside with Monty. I think you'd better go and see him before he causes havoc.'

'Lydia?' Mr Hope was already grabbing his bag. 'It must be bad if she's dragged Monty all the way to the surgery!'

Outside, Lydia was still grappling with Monty. James was standing beside her looking a bit helpless.

'Now, Lydia,' Mr Hope smiled kindly into Lydia's agitated face. 'What's wrong with Monty?'

'He's got a nasty swelling on his back leg,' Lydia said. 'I tried to treat it myself but I'm afraid it's only got worse. *Monty*!' she said angrily. 'Will you please have the good manners to stand still!' Monty ignored his mistress and went on bucking.

'Hmm,' said Mr Hope. 'Let's take a look. Try and hold him still please, Lydia.'

'I'm trying!' Lydia gasped.

Adam Hope couldn't help grinning. He turned to his daughter. 'Give Lydia a hand, will you please, Mandy.'

Mandy put her arms round the goat's neck and gripped tight. She murmured soothing words into his ear. 'Nice Monty, good Monty. Now let Dad take a look at that leg. He won't hurt you, I promise.' The goat tossed his head and rolled his eyes at her. Mandy tried her hardest to keep him steady.

Mr Hope put his bag on the ground and bent to examine one of the animal's hind legs. Then he stood up, looking serious.

'I'm afraid he's got rather a nasty abscess. He's probably been kicked by one of the other goats. Go and ask Simon for the razor and some antibiotics, please, Mandy.'

'OK, Dad.' Mandy let go Monty's neck and dashed back inside. She soon returned with the things her father wanted. Monty seemed to have calmed down a bit and was standing still, trying to eat the hedge.

'Now, hold him steady,' said Mr Hope as Monty eyed him warily. He seemed to know just what Mr Hope intended to do.

Mandy and James helped hold Monty still while Mr Hope quickly shaved the hair from round the abscess.

'Hmm . . . nasty,' Mr Hope mumbled to himself. He took the hypodermic from its sterile pack and inserted the point into a small bottle full of

antibiotic. He drew the liquid into the body of the syringe. 'Right,' he said. 'Here goes.'

He skilfully injected the goat's flank so quickly Monty hardly seemed to notice. The animal didn't flinch. 'There,' said Mr Hope, rubbing the spot where he had stuck the needle in. He stood back, looking satisfied. 'He's as good as gold.'

Then Mr Hope took a small pot from his bag. 'I'll just rub on this ointment to soothe it. There's no need to strangle him, Mandy. I'm sure he'll be fine now.'

But Mr Hope spoke too soon. As he rubbed on the ointment, Monty suddenly kicked out. Mr Hope fell back in surprise, landing in a heap on the path. Mandy and James jumped sideways as the goat took to its heels and galloped off. Lydia was still hanging on to the halter. Blackie barked excitedly, doing his best to drag James after them.

'Thank you very much, Adam!' Lydia shouted over her shoulder, her black wellingtons going like pistons.

By now, goat and owner were halfway across the village green. A line of churned-up turf showed where they had trampled across. Mandy and James collapsed into laughter.

'Are you OK, Dad?' Mandy spluttered as her

father scrambled to his feet. He brushed the dirt from the seat of his jeans.

'Great,' he said looking a bit dazed. 'I don't know what Lydia feeds her goats on – the same stuff racehorses eat I should think!'

Still laughing, all three of them went into Animal Ark. Mandy loved helping her father with his patients. It gave her a great feeling to know she'd had a hand in making them better.

They followed Mr Hope into the surgery and watched while he unpacked his bag and put the used syringe and bottle into the waste bin. He went to the sink and scrubbed his hands.

'Have you heard about Betty's sanctuary having to close?' Mandy asked, sobering up.

'Yes,' Mr Hope said grimly. 'Your mum's been telling me the sad story. Have you decided what to do?'

'Yes,' Mandy said, her eyes shining. 'We're going to have a Grand Novelty Village Pet Show. I'm just going to phone Betty and see what she thinks of the idea.'

Mr Hope raised his eyebrows. 'Well, I think it's a great idea. Where are you going to hold it?'

Mandy glanced at James. She hadn't really thought about where they would hold the show.

'On the village green, I suppose.' she said. 'And we'll need someone to judge the animals. You and Mum will do it, won't you, Dad?'

Mr Hope looked affectionately at his daughter. 'Oh, I should think we could manage that.'

'And we'll need prizes and tables and–' Mandy broke off. She began to feel worried. It had suddenly dawned on her just how much organisation was needed. But she was never one to refuse a challenge.

She jumped off the couch. 'Come on, James. Let's go and phone Betty. Then we'd better make a list of things we need to do.'

'If you're having it on the green, you'll need permission from the parish council,' Mr Hope called as they rushed out.

Mandy came back, looking anxious. 'Why?'

'Well, the green belongs to them. You can't just go holding things on it without permission.'

'OK, then,' said Mandy. 'Who do I ask?'

'Mr Markham,' Adam Hope told her. 'He's the chairman. He lives at number two, The Terrace. I went there yesterday actually – his beagle's got a litter of pups. They're a month old now and needed checking over.'

'Oh, great!' Mandy said, 'Perhaps we'll be able

to see them.' There was nothing she loved more than a litter of puppies.

'Cynthia Markham's very proud of them,' said Mr Hope. 'I'm sure she'll let you.'

Mandy and James went into the house to telephone the sanctuary. Betty answered right away.

'Oh, Mandy, I think that's a really wonderful idea,' she said when Mandy told her about the show. 'If I can do anything to help, please let me know.'

'How's the baby owl?' Mandy asked anxiously.

Betty hesitated. 'I haven't been able to get him to eat anything yet, I'm afraid. I've dug up some worms but he won't take them.'

Mandy's heart sank. 'Oh dear. Perhaps he's not hungry.'

'I think he's still in a state of shock,' Betty said. 'A fall from that height's pretty traumatic. But he's bright and beady-eyed so I'm not too worried about him. He'll soon let me know when he's hungry.'

'I'll come and see him as soon as I can,' Mandy promised.

'Any time,' Betty said. 'And let me know how plans are going for the show.'

'We will.' Mandy put the phone down with a sigh. Then she straightened up. It was pointless worrying about the owl. She knew Betty would do her best with him.

James was waiting in the hall with Blackie.

'Betty thinks the show's a brilliant idea,' Mandy told him. 'Let's go and see Mr Markham and find out if we can hold it on the green!'

The Terrace was a row of pretty Victorian cottages just off the lower high street. Number two had a green-painted front door.

Mandy went boldly up the steps and rang the doorbell.

James tied Blackie to the gate-post and went to join her.

As the door opened, a chorus of barks and yelps came from the end of the long hallway. A grey-haired woman in trousers and a long, striped cardigan stood smiling at Mandy and James.

Mandy swallowed hastily. 'Good morning,' she said with a smile. 'I'm Mandy Hope. Could we see Mr Markham, please?'

Mrs Markham knew straight away who Mandy was. 'Oh, you're the vets' daughter,' she said standing to one side. 'Come on, come in. Have you come to see my Bunty's pups?'

Mandy bit her lip. 'I'd love to,' she told Mrs Markham. 'But could we see your husband first, please? It's very important.'

'Yes, of course,' Mrs Markham said.

'Thanks,' said Mandy. 'This is my friend James Hunter.'

James held out his hand solemnly. 'How do you do,' he said.

The woman shook his hand. 'Can I ask what you want to see my husband about?'

Mandy explained about their plan to raise money for the animal sanctuary.

Mrs Markham looked impressed. 'My, you two, you *are* good. Giving up your time to help Miss Hilder.'

'It's for the sake of the animals,' Mandy said. 'They'll have to be put down and we can't bear the thought of it.'

James shook his head. 'That's right,' he said. 'Betty needs at least five hundred pounds, and we're going to get it for her.'

'My, my, you are determined,' Mrs Markham's voice was full of admiration. She patted James's head as if he were six years old. James gave her a false kind of grin. 'I'm sure my husband will help you if he can,' Mrs Markham went on. 'Come this way, children.'

Mrs Markham led Mandy and James along the carpeted hallway. Through the kitchen door, Mandy spotted a beagle in a huge dog basket feeding a row of six plump puppies. Mandy let out her breath in delight as they passed.

Mrs Markham ushered them into one of the back rooms. A tall, thin man with a bald head sat tapping away at an ancient typewriter. He turned as they entered and peered at them over the top of his spectacles.

'These young people would like to have a word with you about something, Robert,' Mrs Markham explained. 'I'll leave you to it.'

Mandy turned to say thanks but Mrs Markham had bustled away and shut the door behind her.

Mr Markham looked Mandy and James up and down with a stern expression on his face. Mandy felt as if she was standing in front of the head teacher at school.

She had seen Mr Markham before, walking through the village with a clipboard and pen, writing furiously as if he was making notes about everybody. She didn't know how old he was but he looked pretty ancient and *terribly* stern. She suddenly felt very nervous.

Mr Markham continued peering at Mandy and James over the top of his spectacles. A frown creased his shiny brow. Then, suddenly he took off his glasses and smiled. The smile seemed to change his whole face. Little blue eyes sparkled beneath his beetle-brows.

Mandy relaxed. Maybe this interview wasn't going to be so bad after all!

'Well, young people,' Mr Markham put his spectacles down on the desk. 'What can I do for you?'

Mandy explained all over again about the pet show and the animal sanctuary.

To their dismay, Mr Markham shook his head. 'I'm sorry,' he said. 'We just can't do it I'm afraid.'

Mandy tried to hide her disappointment. 'Why not?'

'It's because of that car boot sale the Young Farmers Club held at Easter time, you see.'

Mandy frowned. She didn't see at all. What had a boot sale got to do with a pet show? They weren't *selling* pets, just showing them.

'The grass got so churned up,' Mr Markham explained, 'that the parish council agreed it wouldn't let any more events be held there until next year. I'm sorry, young lady, but you'll have to find somewhere else to have your pet show. Unless you can wait until next year.'

Mandy shook her head. 'We can't. Betty Hilder needs the money *now.*'

Mr Markham shook his head again. 'Sorry. There's nothing I can do.'

He stood up and went with them to the door. 'If you do find somewhere suitable, let me know,' he said. 'I'd like to bring Bunty along. I'm sure she'd win a prize.'

'Oh, yes, please do bring her,' Mandy said enthusiastically. Trying to swallow her disappointment she led the way along the hallway towards the kitchen where Mrs Markham was giving the beagle a drink of milk. The puppies were playing on the rug, barking and tumbling and having mock battles with one another.

'Come on in,' she called to Mandy and James, who were hesitating in the doorway. It didn't seem quite polite to go barging into the room without being asked.

Mandy went in and sat down on the floor. Seeing the litter of puppies had cheered her up.

'They're absolutely gorgeous,' she said, holding

one gently up to her cheek. She felt the warm, soft fur against her skin. The puppy squirmed and tried to get a mouthful of her hair. Mandy laughed and put him down with his brothers and sisters. He ran off, his roly-poly body wobbling, and disappeared under the kitchen table.

Mrs Markham sighed. 'Yes, I'll really miss them when they have to go.'

'Have you found homes for them all?' asked James, playing tag with a puppy with a pretty brown face and floppy ears.

Mrs Markham nodded. 'Yes, I advertised them in the local paper. They were soon snapped up.'

'Not like those poor dogs at the sanctuary,' Mandy said sadly, getting up, ready to leave.

'Was my husband able to help you?' Mrs Markham said as she went with them to the front door.

Mandy shook her head sadly. 'No. He said an event like that would churn up the grass too much.'

'Oh, dear,' said Mrs Markham. 'I remember what the green looked like after that boot sale last year. It was more like a ploughed field than a village green. Did my husband have any other suggestions?'

Mandy shook her head again. 'No, not really.'

'I am sorry,' Mrs Markham said. 'Let me know if you have any luck finding somewhere else.' Then, suddenly, her face lit up. 'I know,' she said. 'Why don't you ask Amelia Ponsonby?'

'Mrs *Ponsonby*!' Mandy and James chorused.

'Yes,' said Mrs Markham. 'Do you know her?'

Mandy and James stared at each other. They had had dealings with Mrs Ponsonby before. In fact, there was hardly anyone in the village who *hadn't* had dealings with Mrs Ponsonby one way or another. The woman made it her business to know everything and everyone in Welford!

'Do we *know* her?' James chuckled. 'Everybody knows Mrs Ponsonby.'

'Well then,' said Mrs Markham. 'Why not ask her if you can have the show at her house? Bleakfell Hall is huge and it has a great big garden. I know Mrs Ponsonby's very fond of animals. And she did adopt a dog from Betty's sanctuary. She might be willing to let you hold it there.'

Mandy looked thoughtful. Maybe Mrs Markham was right. Maybe Mrs Ponsonby *would* let them hold the show at Bleakfell Hall.

But James looked dubious. 'She's a bit of a fuss-pot,' he said.

'Well, it's up to you,' said Mrs Markham. 'It could be worth a try.'

They said goodbye. James untied Blackie from the gate-post and they headed off towards the village green.

'Well,' said James, seeing Mandy's thoughtful face. 'Are we going to ask Mrs Ponsonby or not?'

'Yes,' Mandy said matter-of-factly. 'Remember when she adopted her little mongrel, Toby?'

'Yes,' said James.

'Well, then we know she really cares about homeless animals. Come on, let's give it a try!'

Four

Mandy and James ran down the street and across the green towards Animal Ark, Blackie at their heels. They rushed round the back to get their bikes.

Mrs Hope came to the gate. 'Where are you two off to?'

'We're going up to Bleakfell Hall to ask Mrs Ponsonby if we can hold the pet show there,' Mandy explained hastily.

'Can I leave Blackie here, please?' James asked.

Mrs Hope took hold of the Labrador's lead. 'Yes, of course. I'll put him in the kitchen.' She pulled a wry face. 'Good luck with Mrs Ponsonby – you're going to need it!'

'Thanks, Mum,' said Mandy.

'And don't be a nuisance now,' Mrs Hope called as they pedalled away. 'Mrs Ponsonby's a very busy woman!'

They cycled pell-mell through the village. Outside the post office Mrs McFarlane was talking to the postman.

'You two are in a hurry,' she called as she saw Mandy and James speeding past.

'We're on urgent business,' James called as they pedalled by.

Halfway up to Bleakfell Hall, Mandy's courage began to fail. She slowed down and waited for James to pedal alongside her.

'What do you think she'll say?' she asked, suddenly feeling they might be on a wild goose chase.

James bit his lip. 'I don't know,' he said. 'She's awfully bossy. She might not give us a chance to tell her what it's all about.'

'Yes, I know.' said Mandy. Then she thought about Betty and the animals, and drew a deep breath. 'Well,' she said, 'we're going to ask her. She won't bite our heads off, will she?'

'She might,' said James. He had always been a bit scared of Mrs Ponsonby. She was so huge and had *such* a loud voice!

Mandy laughed at his dismal face and punched him playfully on the shoulder. 'Chin up, James. Mrs Ponsonby might be a fuss-pot but she's not a monster. Come on, I'll race you.'

'If you say so,' James mumbled.

Mandy sped on ahead. She pedalled over the bridge, and through the stone gateway, then up the long gravel drive towards the imposing front door. Bleakfell Hall was a huge grey-stone Victorian mansion with tall chimneys and towers and turrets.

To Mandy's dismay, one wing was completely encased in scaffolding. Mrs Ponsonby obviously had the builders in.

Mandy skidded to a halt on the gravel.

'Oh, no,' she said disappointedly. 'Builders!'

'She won't want to be bothered with us by the looks of it,' said James, looking crestfallen.

Mandy took a deep breath. 'Well, as we've come all this way, we might as well ask anyway.' Mandy wasn't one to be easily put off.

They leaned their bikes against one of the stone pillars that flanked the front steps and went to press the old-fashioned bell-push beside the front door.

The housekeeper answered. She was a tiny woman in an apron almost to her ankles.

'Could we see Mrs Ponsonby, please?' Mandy asked politely.

'Who shall I say is calling?' asked the housekeeper.

'Er . . . Mandy Hope and James Hunter,' said Mandy.

'Please wait here.' The housekeeper scuttled away along a dim corridor towards the kitchen and disappeared inside muttering to herself.

After about five minutes Mrs Ponsonby came sailing down the stairs in a tweed suit and sensible shoes. She wore a green felt hat with a feather in it over her blue-rinsed hair. Mrs Ponsonby was very fond of her hats and had one to suit every occasion. In fact, Mandy couldn't remember ever having seen her in the same hat twice. Tucked under her arm was a pale-cream Pekinese dog with tiny black, boot-button eyes. Scampering behind came Toby, a little brown mongrel. He ran up to Mandy and James barking, his tail wagging furiously. He jumped up at Mandy. She bent down to stroke him.

'Hello, Toby,' she said, tickling the little dog behind the ear. 'You look well.' She was pleased to see the little dog looking so healthy. When Betty Hilder had first brought Toby to Animal Ark, he had been abandoned with a broken leg.

Mrs Ponsonby looked very surprised to see them standing there. She peered at them through the lenses of her pink spectacles.

'Who on earth let you in?' she said loudly.

'Er . . . a lady. I think she was the housekeeper,' said Mandy in a small voice. She gazed up at Mrs Ponsonby. The woman looked larger than ever, standing above Mandy, staring down at her.

Mrs Ponsonby frowned and tutted. 'That woman is hopeless, isn't she?' she said, more to the Pekinese than to Mandy and James. 'She's probably forgotten all about you already. You could have been standing here all day.' She reached the bottom stair. 'Well, what can I do for you?' she asked. 'I'm afraid I can't cope with any more dogs, Mandy.'

'Oh, no,' Mandy assured her hastily. 'It's not that. It's something else.'

'Well?' Mrs Ponsonby raised her eyebrows.

Mandy straightened up. 'We came here to ask you a favour,' she said with determination.

Mrs Ponsonby looked suspicious. 'A favour?'

'Yes,' Mandy said breathlessly. Then she quickly explained their scheme.

Mrs Ponsonby put Pandora down on the floor. The Pekinese waddled off.

'Pandora!' called Mrs Ponsonby. 'Pandora, come back!'

Toby followed the peke. They both ignored their mistress.

When Mandy had finished explaining, Mrs Ponsonby shook her head. The feather on her hat waved about just like Pandora's tail. 'I couldn't possibly let everyone run riot in my grounds.'

'They won't run riot,' James said. 'We'll have things properly organised. Mr and Mrs Hope are going to help and I'm sure my mum and dad will too.'

Mrs Ponsonby shook her head again. 'No. It's bad enough with the builders and their great boots. I'm afraid you'll have to find somewhere else. I'd like to help but it's impossible.' She looked at them not unkindly. 'I'd be pleased to enter Pandora and Toby.' She sniffed. 'Of course, they'll win every class they enter.'

Mandy sighed and tried not to look too disappointed. 'Oh well, thanks, Mrs Ponsonby.

We'll just have to find somewhere else.'

Mrs Ponsonby escorted them to the door. 'I was just going to see Mr Western about all the mud his tractors leave on the road,' she said. 'My car gets *filthy* when I drive past his place. I *could* have a word with him about Miss Hilder's rent. He's put it up, you say?'

'Yes,' Mandy said mournfully. 'And Betty can't possibly afford to pay it and have the animal shelters repaired *and* buy food as well.'

'I'll have to find out what's going on,' said Mrs Ponsonby. She liked to know everyone's business. 'Goodbye, children,' she called as they walked forlornly down the steps.

Mandy and James got on their bikes and rode slowly down the drive.

'She didn't even say sorry,' James said grumpily.

'I know,' Mandy said with a sigh. She felt really sad. Would they ever find anywhere to hold the show? 'Oh, James,' she said miserably. '*Now* what are we going to do?'

'Go home and think,' said James.

Mandy and James arrived back at Animal Ark and sat round the kitchen table drinking Cokes.

'We could ask our headmaster if we could have

the pet show at school,' James suggested hopefully.

Mandy shook her head. 'That's no good. We want the show here in the village, don't we? It's the *Welford* sanctuary. It's got to be the *Welford* show.'

James scratched his ear. 'Hey,' he said suddenly. 'What about the Parker Smythes? They've got a great big garden *and* an indoor swimming-pool – we could have dog swimming races!'

Mandy pulled a face. 'The Parker Smythes? I don't think that's a very good idea. You know how stuck-up they are.'

'Well,' said James, 'Mrs Parker Smythe loves showing off. You know she does. If we held the show there, everyone in the village would be able to see her posh house and posh swimming-pool, wouldn't they?'

'Hmm . . .' said Mandy. 'That's true. I hadn't thought of that.'

'And she loves bragging about Mr Parker Smythe being a producer on telly,' James went on. 'She could tell everyone that too.'

Mandy decided it was worth a try. She jumped up. 'OK, James. You've convinced me! Let's go and ask.'

The Parker Smythes lived in Beacon House, a

huge, white mansion set high up on Beacon Hill. It looked down on the rest of the village just as Mrs Parker Smythe looked down on its inhabitants.

Mandy and James rode up there in no time at all.

Outside the mansion's high security gates, Mandy's heart sank. The notice 'Trespassers will be prosecuted' seemed a bad omen. Maybe it had been a mistake to come here. The huge gates and the notice hardly welcomed people to the house.

Mandy sat astride her bike with her feet on the ground. She looked at James. 'What do you think?'

James shrugged and took off his glasses. He polished them on the knee of his jeans then put them back on. 'I don't know,' he said.

Mandy chewed her lip. It was really important that they got the pet show organised as soon as possible. They had got to find somewhere to have the show. This could be their very last chance.

Mandy combed her hair back with her fingers and squared her shoulders determinedly. She had made up her mind to give it a try.

'Well,' she said to James. 'Here goes!'

She stood on tiptoe and pressed a button on the security intercom attached to one of the pillars. There was a hiss and a popping noise and a squeaky voice asked who was there.

Mandy told the machine and after another click the huge gates swung silently open. It was like getting permission to enter a prison!

Mandy and James cycled along the drive, through the little spinney and between neat hedges that led up to the front door. Their ring on the bell was answered straight away.

A short, overweight girl stood dwarfed by the huge door frame. She was dressed in bright pink Lycra leggings and a white fluffy jumper with a kitten embroider on the front. She had chocolate all round her mouth.

'Yes?' she asked. 'Have you come to play with me?' Her tongue came out as she tried to lick the chocolate off.

'Hi, Imogen,' Mandy said brightly. Imogen was the spoiled seven-year-old daughter of the Parker Smythes.

'Is your mum in?' James piped up.

'She's in the sauna,' said Imogen, as if taking a sauna was the most ordinary thing in the world.

'A sauna!' James spluttered beside Mandy.

Mandy nudged him. There was only one way to deal with Imogen and that was to be as sweet as pie.

'Any idea how long she'll be?' she asked the little girl gently.

Imogen wriggled around as if she had a scorpion in her knickers. 'Yes,' she said. 'Ages probably. She and Daddy went to a party last night and Mummy's recovering.'

'Oh,' said Mandy, not knowing quite what else to say.

'But come in and play with me,' Imogen insisted. 'Daddy's bought me a new doll's-house and I've got a new video and lots of–'

Just then Mrs Parker Smythe came through into the hallway. Mandy sighed with relief. She'd thought Imogen would never stop.

Mrs Parker Smythe was swathed from head to immaculately painted scarlet toenail in a pure white, fluffy, towelling robe. Her blonde hair was covered by a peach coloured turban.

'Who is it, Immie darling?' she enquired.

'Mandy Hope and James Hunter,' Imogen replied. 'They've come to play with me.'

'Er . . . no,' Mandy said. 'Sorry, we actually wanted to see your mum.'

Imogen stuck out her bottom lip in a sulk. 'It's not fair,' she moaned. 'No one ever comes to play with me.'

'I'm not surprised,' James whispered to Mandy.

Mrs Parker Smythe tottered towards them across the marble floor. She wore white satin high-heeled mules that slipped and slithered as if the floor was covered with ice.

She stared at Mandy. 'You're the vets' daughter, aren't you?'

'Yes,' Mandy confirmed. She went on talking quickly. She knew if she let Mrs Parker Smythe get a word in edgeways she would hear grand tales of her husband's involvement in television, the famous people that came to stay in Beacon House and stories of how brilliant dear Immie was at all kinds of things from playing the piano to tap-dancing.

When Mandy finished telling Mrs Parker Smythe why they were there, the woman sat down heavily on one of the gold brocade chaise-longues that lined the sparkling hallway.

'I'm not sure my husband would relish the idea of the hoi polloi coming up here in droves,' she said.

'What's hoi polloi?' James whispered in Mandy's ear.

'No idea,' Mandy whispered back.

Mrs Parker Smythe looked at them as if they

were something that had crawled from the woodwork. 'Hoi polloi,' she said, obviously overhearing. 'Villagers . . . you know, *common* people.'

'But you would love them to see your gorgeous house, wouldn't you?' said Mandy. 'And your lovely garden. Your husband could even make a film of the event.' She turned to Imogen, 'You could be the star, Imogen.'

Imogen began to jump up and down waving her fat fists in the air. 'Yes Mummy, yes Mummy, yes Mummy,' she chanted.

Mrs Parker Smythe passed her hand across her eyes. 'Immie darling, I've got the most dreadful headache.' She looked slightly bewildered.

Imogen ran up to her and banged her on the knee. 'I want the pet show here!' she shouted. 'I want to be a film star!'

Mandy glanced at James and could see he was tempted to throw darling Immie into the Parker Smythes' posh indoor swimming-pool.

Mrs Parker Smythe was trying to calm her daughter down. 'Very well, dear,' she was saying. 'We'll have a little pet show if that's what you want.' She glanced up at Mandy and James. 'But it will have to be dear little bunnies and kittens and

things like that. I can't have great big dogs trampling over my beautiful Persian rugs.'

'The animals wouldn't have to come indoors,' Mandy assured her.

Mrs Parker Smythe waved her hand. 'Well, they might make messes on the lawn. We've got the famous Italian film director Mario Ponti coming next week. Can you imagine him treading . . .' She shuddered. 'I couldn't take the risk. Just bunnies and kitties.'

'And mice?' James asked innocently.

Mandy almost laughed out loud. At the mention of the word 'mice' Mrs Parker Smythe gave a little scream. Her turban wobbled and slipped to one side. 'Mice! You aren't serious?'

Mandy couldn't resist taking it further. 'Oh, yes,' she said. 'If it's only to be *small* pets, there'll be mice, gerbils, spiders, rats . . .'

For one minute Mandy thought Mrs Parker Smythe was going to faint. She went almost as pale as her robe. They'd blown their chances of holding the pet show at Beacon House, that was for sure!

Mrs Parker Smythe stood up shakily and took hold of Mandy and James's elbows. She steered them quickly to the front door. 'No, I'm sorry,' she breathed. 'I think perhaps you'd better find somewhere else to have your pet show. I'd be quite happy to give a donation to the sanctuary.' She shuddered again. 'But mice . . . and *rats* . . . oh dear, I feel quite faint. I think I'll go and have a lie-down.'

She pushed Mandy and James through the door and shut it firmly behind them. In the hall, Imogen began to shout and scream, 'I want mice, I want mice, I want mice!'

James took the lead. He grabbed Mandy's arm. 'Come on, let's go.'

Still giggling they tore off down the drive. The huge gates opened as if by magic and they were through, pedalling back down the hill towards the village. Mandy threw back her head and laughed. Mrs Parker Smythe's expression when they mentioned the mice had been a picture!

'Did you see her face?' Mandy chortled. 'Oh dear, poor Mrs Parker Smythe, she'll have nightmares for a week. Whose idea was it to go there, James?'

'Mine,' James said sheepishly. 'Sorry.'

Mandy stopped her bike and looked at the wide sweeps of moorland, and the blue sky with just a few cotton-wool clouds drifting slowly across the tops of the hills. She heaved a sigh. She felt disappointed. But holding a pet show at Beacon House would never have worked. They'd just have to find somewhere else.

'It's OK, James,' she said. 'We're not giving up yet. Come on. Let's get back and see what other bright ideas we can come up with, shall we?'

When they reached the village, James went into the post office to get some sherbet lemons while Mandy waited outside. When James came out, they parked their bikes by the village seat and sat down. The village seat was always a good place to sit and think. Mandy's mind was racing. They'd tried three things now and nothing was working out. She began to feel desperate. Someone, somewhere, must be willing to host the show.

The Reverend Hadcroft came cycling down the road on his old black bicycle. He went into the post office and came out with the daily paper under his arm.

'Hello, you two,' he called. 'You look down in the dumps.'

'We are,' James called.

The vicar strolled over and sat beside them. He was a young man with a shock of black hair and bright blue eyes.

'OK,' he said. 'Tell me what's up.'

Between them they told him their story.

Mr Hadcroft frowned and fiddled thoughtfully with the edge of his cassock. 'It seems to me,' he said wisely, 'that you two are making a mountain out of a molehill.'

A mountain out of a molehill! Mandy thought indignantly. Saving the animal sanctuary was just about the most important thing in the world right at that moment!

'What do you mean?' she asked, puzzled.

The vicar grinned broadly. 'Well,' he said, 'why not hold it in the vicarage garden? If it's good enough for the Women's Institute to hold their summer fête, then it's good enough for you to hold a pet show, isn't it?'

Mandy's heart leaped. The vicarage garden would be excellent! It had a big square lawn with lots of places to put tables and mark out parade rings. It would be just brilliant!

'Oh, wow, Mr Hadcroft,' she said excitedly. 'Could we?'

Mr Hadcroft grinned. 'Yes, why not?'

Mandy leapt to her feet. 'Oh, that would be really great. Thanks, Mr Hadcroft.' She felt like hugging him but wasn't quite sure if it would be the right thing to do. She turned to James, her eyes shining.

'Come on, James. There's lots to do.' They were going to have an incredibly busy half-term holiday, that was for sure!

There was a twinkle in the vicar's eye as he stood up with them. 'Of course,' he said, 'I'll need a donation for the church roof fund if I'm going to let you use my garden.'

Mandy's face fell. She knew how badly the church needed a new roof, but animals needed roofs over their heads too. 'Oh . . .' she said, trying not to sound too glum. She winced. 'How much?'

The vicar clasped his hands together in front of him and raised his eyes to the sky as if he was asking for guidance. Finally he looked at Mandy and James.

'Shall we say one pound? Could you manage that?'

Mandy stared at him. Then a huge grin broke over her face. Mr Hadcroft was as bad as her dad for teasing!

She beamed him a smile. 'I'm sure we could manage a pound, aren't you, James?'

'Absolutely,' said James.

'Great!' exclaimed Mr Hadcroft. 'You'd better come and see me later when you've made some more plans. I'll do anything to help you, of course.'

'We will,' Mandy called as they pushed their bikes hurriedly towards Animal Ark. All of a sudden she felt wonderful. She might have known they would succeed in finding somewhere. In a village like Welford there was always *someone* to lend a helping hand.

Mandy's mind was already whirling, planning their next move. She wanted to make the Grand Novelty Village Pet Show an event that no one would ever forget!

Five

Mandy and James dashed excitedly back towards Animal Ark to tell the Hopes the good news. Mandy was already thinking up ideas. They'd need tables, prizes, someone to–

Suddenly a green car swung round the corner. At the same time, it seemed from out of nowhere, a beautiful tan and black German Shepherd streaked across the green. It careered straight into the road. There was nothing the car driver could do to avoid it. There was a loud, ominous screech of brakes and a sickening thud as the front bumper hit the dog.

Mandy skidded to a halt and dropped her bike.

Her hands flew to her mouth. For a moment she froze in horror.

'Oh, no!'

Heart thudding with fear, Mandy sprang forward. The dog was lying motionless on its side in the road. The driver, a woman in her twenties, had got out and was standing looking at it, shaking her head. Tears were running down her face. She wrung her hands together in despair.

'She just ran out. There was nothing I could do!' the woman wailed.

'I know,' Mandy gasped. 'I saw her. Don't worry. It wasn't your fault.'

The young woman looked at Mandy with an agonised face. She knelt down beside the unconscious dog. 'What on earth shall we do?'

Then a young man in a black leather jacket appeared from round the corner. He had longish, thick, blond hair and a tanned face with startling blue eyes. 'Sheba!' he shouted desperately. 'Sheba!'

His eyes widened in horror when he saw what had happened.

He rushed over and knelt down beside Mandy. He rocked backwards and forwards on his heels. There were tears in his eyes as he glanced at her.

'She ran away from me,' he said, looking distraught.

'I'm so sorry,' the young woman said, wiping her eyes. 'I couldn't avoid her. She just ran out.'

'I saw it all,' Mandy said quickly. 'It couldn't be helped.'

The young man stretched his hand to touch the dog.

'No, don't touch her!' Mandy said hastily. Her mind was racing. The dog was still breathing, but unconscious. There was no sign of any blood but it would be a mistake to touch or move Sheba until either Mr or Mrs Hope had taken a look at her.

Mandy quickly shrugged off her jacket. She laid it very gently over the animal. 'I'll get help.' She turned to James. 'Don't let anyone move her,' she said urgently.

Then she was off, racing towards Animal Ark, her heart pounding. She knew the rules of first aid. Keep the animal warm, look for signs of bleeding, of broken limbs. But her mum or dad were the ones to help. People who didn't know what they were up to might do more harm than good.

Mandy flew in the surgery door. It hit the wall with a bang.

Jean Knox was just about to protest when she saw Mandy's white face.

'Where's Mum or Dad?' Mandy cried.

'In the house . . .' Jean began. But Mandy had already disappeared. She dashed through the surgery and into the kitchen.

Mr Hope was ironing his white surgery coat. He looked up in surprise as Mandy ran in.

'Quick, Dad. A dog's been knocked down!'

Mr Hope quickly switched off the iron and ran to get a blanket and his bag. He sped down the path after Mandy.

In the road, James was standing with his arms out to warn any oncoming traffic. For once, Blackie sat obediently by his feet. The young man was talking to James.

'My uncle will kill me!' he said. He sat on the kerb with his head in his hands.

'Your uncle?' asked James, waving a motorcyclist past.

'Yes, I'm staying with him at Moon Cottage. Sheba's his dog. I begged him to let me take her out. I love dogs but I live in the city and you can't keep a dog in a flat.'

Mandy arrived just in time to hear him explaining. Her heart lurched with sympathy. She knew how hard it was to control a dog like a German Shepherd if you weren't used to them.

The young man looked up. Relief crossed his face when he saw Mr Hope's leather bag.

'This is my dad,' explained Mandy, 'He's a vet. Sheba will be OK now, don't worry.'

But Mandy sounded more confident than she felt. The dog was still unconscious and her breathing was shallow. One hind leg lay at a crooked angle. Mandy could only pray it wasn't broken. Then, horrified, she noticed blood seeping from Sheba's lower jaw. Her stomach turned over. 'Dad!' she cried. 'Look!'

Mr Hope's face was grim as he knelt down beside the unconscious animal. He took out his stethoscope and listened to the dog's heart and lungs.

'They seem OK,' he said, sounding relieved. He replaced the stethoscope then gently lifted the dog's upper lip and pressed a finger against her gum. When he took it away, the gum immediately went pink again although his finger was covered in blood.

Mr Hope looked up. 'If the gum hadn't gone pink,' he explained, 'it would have meant she had internal bleeding. Luckily that seems OK. The blood's just where her teeth have pierced her lip.' He pulled the dog's eyelids open and looked into her pupils. 'She's definitely in shock. Let's hope that's all.'

He quickly examined the dog's limbs. 'Umm,' he muttered, touching the crooked hind leg. 'I spoke too soon. This one's broken, I'm afraid. Let's get her back to the surgery before she wakes up.'

Mandy helped her dad spread the blanket out on the tarmac.

'Help me,' Mr Hope said to the young man. 'And be careful,' he warned. 'If she comes round, she might bite.'

Gently supporting the dog's head and body, they lifted her on to the blanket to use it as a makeshift stretcher. Mr Hope made sure the dog's neck was extended so her breathing wasn't obstructed.

Mandy and James trailed behind as Mr Hope and the young man carried Sheba over to Animal Ark.

'Poor Sheba,' James said mournfully.

'If it's just a broken leg, she'll be OK,' said Mandy. 'Dad'll plaster it up then keep her at the Ark to make sure there's nothing worse wrong with her.'

Back at Animal Ark, Mandy and James sat in

the waiting-room with the young man. In the surgery, Mr Hope and Simon gave Sheba a more thorough examination and put her leg into plaster.

The young man introduced himself. 'I'm Mark Boston,' he said. 'I'm looking for a house to buy in Welford. It's such a great place.' He shook his head. 'I don't know if my uncle will want me living near him after this.'

Mandy tried to cheer him up. 'It really wasn't your fault,' she insisted. She suddenly realised she hadn't seen the car driver since she had rushed to get her dad. 'What happened to the woman driving the car?'

'She had to meet her kids from school,' Mark explained. 'She said she'd call in later to see how Sheba was. She felt terrible.'

'So did I,' James piped up. 'I thought Sheba was dead.'

'Don't even think about it!' Mark shook his head. He turned to Mandy. 'I don't know what I'd have done without your help, Mandy. I'm really grateful.'

Mandy shrugged. 'It's a good job we were there,' she said, 'I'd have done the same for any animal.' Her face lit up. 'I want to be a vet too.'

'Well, I'm sure you'll make a great one.'

Just then, Mr Hope came through, drying his hands on a towel.

Mark jumped up anxiously. Mr Hope put a reassuring hand on his arm. 'Now, don't panic. She's going to be OK.'

Mandy felt relief wash over her. Mark looked relieved too. He sat back down heavily. Colour flooded back into his cheeks. 'Is it just her leg?'

'I'm pretty sure that's all that's wrong with her, but I'll keep her under observation. You'd better go and tell your uncle what's happened.'

Mark pulled a worried face. 'He's going to kill me,' he repeated. 'I know he is.'

We'll come with you if you like,' volunteered Mandy. 'We can tell him it wasn't your fault.'

Mark smiled down at her. 'The thing is, Mandy, it *was* my fault. I should have had her on a lead.' He sighed. 'No, I've got to face the music.' Then he laughed loudly although Mandy couldn't quite see what was so funny.

Mark went on. 'If I do come to live near here,' he said, 'I want a house with lots of land so I can keep some animals. You two will have to come and give me a few hints on how to look after them.'

'We'd love to,' Mandy said. She liked Mark a lot.

Anyone who was fond of animals was OK in Mandy's book. And, it was very strange, she had the feeling that she'd seen Mark somewhere before.

'Excellent,' James said with a grin. He patted Blackie. 'You can practise on Blackie if you like.'

Mark smiled. 'I think I'd better have a few lessons first.'

'Have you been to Welford before?' Mandy asked. She was still puzzling over where she might have seen him.

Mark nodded. 'Years ago, when I was a kid about your age. I never forgot what a great place it was. I always had this dream of living in the country, and now I've got the money to do just that.'

They went through to see Sheba. She was awake now, sitting on the floor, licking her newly-plastered leg. She looked groggy and very sorry for herself.

'I've given her a sedative,' said Mr Hope. 'She's bound to be bruised and sore. We'll put her out in the recovery room.'

'Will she try to get the plaster off?' asked Mark.

'She might,' said Mr Hope. 'If she carries on worrying at it, we'll have to put a plastic cone over her head so she can't get at it. Let's see how she gets on first. Some dogs accept the plaster in no time at all and hop around as if they've worn it all their lives.'

Mark crouched down and fondled Sheba's head. She managed a feeble wag of her tail.

'I'm sorry, old girl,' Mark said, his voice breaking. After a minute or two he stood up, squaring his broad shoulders. 'I expect Clive, my uncle, will want to come and see her. Is that OK?'

'Of course,' said Mr Hope. 'And it'll probably be OK to pick her up this time tomorrow.'

Mark shook his hand. 'Thanks, I'm really grateful.'

'Just part of the job,' Mr Hope said. 'It's lucky

Mandy was there. If anyone had tried to move Sheba it could have caused more injury.'

'I know,' Mark said. He put his arm round Mandy and gave her a hug. 'I'll buy you a Coke sometime, Mandy, and you, James.'

Mr Hope went out with Mark, discussing fees. 'I'll pay, of course,' Mark was saying.

Mandy stood watching. Then a frown creased her brow. She chewed her lip. 'You know, James,' she said thoughtfully. 'I've seen Mark somewhere before.'

'If he came to stay in the village you might have seen him then,' James suggested.

'Maybe,' said Mandy. 'But I'd only have been a little kid. No, I've seen him recently but I just can't think where!'

When the excitement and worry of the injured dog was over, Mandy and James sat at the kitchen table with pencil and paper, making plans for the Grand Novelty Village Pet Show.

'We'll need to make some notices,' said James. He was good at that kind of thing.

'Yes,' Mandy agreed. It was vital that as many people as possible knew when and where the show would be held.

'But when *are* we going to have it?' asked James. 'We haven't decided yet.'

'Saturday's best,' said Mandy. 'When people are home from work.'

'Right,' said James. 'Next Saturday?'

'Yes,' she said quickly. 'Let's make it next Saturday!'

'We'd better ask Mr Hadcroft if that day's OK,' said James.

'Good idea,' Mandy jumped up. 'I'll phone him now.'

She came back smiling. 'Saturday's fine,' she said. 'Mr Hadcroft wondered if we'd have everything organised in time but I said we would.'

'Great,' said James. 'Right, let's make that list. First we'll need prizes.'

Mandy gulped. 'Prizes! Of course. Where are we going to get those from?'

James bit the end of his pencil. 'Um . . . I don't know.'

'I could ask Walter Pickard. He loves animals. He might find something we could give as a prize.'

'Right,' James scribbled away. 'We could just walk round the village and ask people them if they'll donate a prize. Does that sound like a good idea?'

'Brilliant,' said Mandy. 'I'm sure there's lots of people who'd give something.'

'Right,' said James. 'Now we need to decide what competitions we're going to have. Then we'll need tables, and cages and judges and a loudspeaker and . . .'

Mandy stared at him. Tables, cages . . . It looked as if finding the venue and prizes were only the first of a long line of problems they had to solve.

The door opened and Simon came through to put the kettle on. 'What's this?' he asked, peering over James's shoulder.

'A list of stuff we need for our pet show,' said James.

'You haven't got "marquee" on it,' said Simon.

Mandy gulped. 'What do we need a marquee for?'

'In case it rains, of course. You can't trust the weather this time of year. You can't parade animals round in the pouring rain. They'll end up looking like drowned rats.'

Mandy's face fell. Simon was right. She hadn't thought of that. Where on earth were they going to get a marquee from?

'The scouts have got one!' James said suddenly.

'Maybe they'd let us borrow it.'

'It would cost you,' said Simon, putting some tea into the pot. 'Loads of money.'

Mandy looked at him sideways. She had already promised her pocket money to Betty for the owl's food. Where on earth was she going to get the money to hire a marquee? Then she noticed Simon was grinning. 'You're joking, aren't you?'

'Well, maybe not loads of money but they do charge to hire it out.'

Mandy sighed. This was all becoming very complicated. But she wasn't going to be put off. Gran always said nothing was worth doing unless it was worth doing well.

'Anyway,' Simon was waiting for the tea to brew, 'why don't you ask Jean? She's friends with Mrs Browne, the scout leader. She might put in a good word for you.'

'Great, thanks, Simon. If she's Jean's friend she might let us have it for nothing!' Mandy was going to jump up to ask Jean that very minute but James held her arm.

'Hang on,' he said. 'Let's get this list done.'

Mandy sat down again. 'OK – what next?'

'The competitions.'

Mandy raised her eyebrows thoughtfully. 'Right . . . er, how about the dog with the waggiest tail?'

Simon was just pouring out mugs of tea for himself and Jean. He laughed when he heard Mandy's suggestion.

'I reckon Blackie would win that,' Simon said. He picked up the mugs and walked towards the door. 'You've got to give everyone a fair chance, you know. No favouritism.'

'We will,' Mandy said indignantly. 'That's why we're having all kinds of different classes.'

'How about the cat with the longest whiskers, then,' Simon suggested.

James scribbled away. 'Great. What else?'

'I'm sure you two will think of something.' Simon said. He pushed the door open with his foot. 'If you need any more suggestions, let me know.'

'Thanks, Simon,' Mandy said. She was still racking her brains. What kind of pets did her village friends have?

There were cats and dogs of course. Old Ernie Bell who lived near Mr Pickard had a pet squirrel. There were rabbits and guinea-pigs and she knew of at least two of her school friends who kept rats as pets. Mandy chuckled. She only had to think of the word 'rat' and she could see the chocolate-covered Imogen Parker Smythe and her poor mother's expression of horror.

There were bound to be other pets as well. Pets like budgies, parrots, stick insects, goldfish. The list was endless.

'How about the rodent with the twitchiest nose,' she suggested to James. 'That'll cover gerbils, hamsters, mice and *rats*!'

'*Rats*!' James screeched, imitating Mrs Parker Smythe, 'Oh, no, not *rats*!'

Mandy laughed. 'What else can you think of? We're not getting very far.'

'How about the most disobedient dog?' he suggested, pushing his glasses back up his nose.

'You're thinking of Blackie again,' said Mandy.

James looked indignant. 'No, I'm not. What about Pandora and Toby? Did you see the way they ignored Mrs Ponsonby this morning?'

Mandy grinned. 'I certainly did. Those dogs are wonderful at ignoring Mrs Ponsonby. They're the only ones who can!'

James laughed. 'Shall I put that on the list, then?'

Mandy nodded. 'Sure, yes, go ahead. It'll be

much more fun than the most *obedient* one. And that's what we want – people to have . . . fun!'

James was scribbling with fury. 'What else? We need about ten in all.'

'The most talkative budgie?' suggested Mandy.

'Excellent,' said James, adjusting his glasses again.

'Right,' Mandy looked thoughtful. 'Hmm . . .'

'The stickiest stick insect?' James suggested.

'Now you *are* being silly,' Mandy laughed.

The list was growing rapidly – the best rescued dog or cat, the best turned-out pet, the most unusual pet.

'My friend at school's got a pet woodlouse,' said James. 'I bet that would win.'

To round it off they decided on the dog who can eat his dinner fastest and the most scruffy pet in Welford.

They sat back looking pleased with themselves.

'Now,' said Mandy. 'The prizes.'

'And someone to present them,' added James.

Mandy bit her lip. She'd forgotten all about that. What they needed was someone famous. Someone who would really draw the crowds. Who on earth could they find? Suddenly, she had an idea. 'What about Susan Collins's mum?'

Susan and Mrs Collins lived in a big house on the road to Walton. Mrs Collins used to act in *Parson's Close*, a soap opera on TV, and still did a little acting from time to time. Her professional name was Miranda Jones.

James's eyes lit up. 'Brilliant! Give her a ring!'

She hurried out into the hall to use the phone. Minutes later, she came back looking crestfallen.

'She said she'd love to but she's got to visit her aunt in hospital on Saturday.'

James stuck his elbows on the table. 'Never mind,' he said. 'Maybe we'll think of someone else. I'll go home now and do the notices. Then we'll take them round the village tomorrow and ask people about prizes.'

'Good idea,' said Mandy. 'I can't wait!'

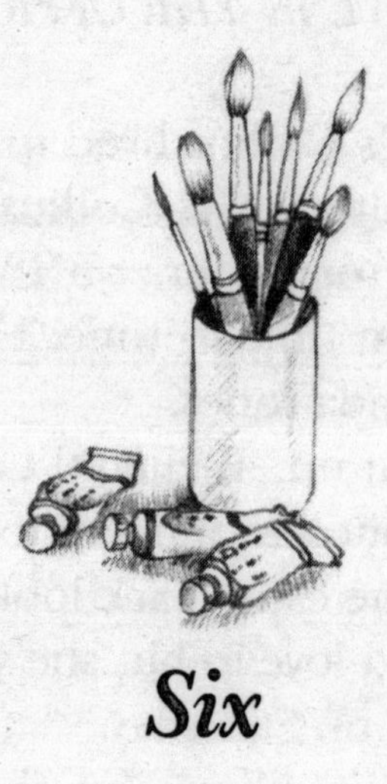

Six

Just as James was going out, there was a knock at the back door.

When Mandy opened it, a tall man with black hair and a beard stood on the step. He looked very upright and rather stern but when he spoke he had a kind and gentle voice. He wore jeans and an open-necked shirt with a bright scarf tied at the collar.

Although he was a relative newcomer to the village Mandy had seen the man several times before. He was a painter and he often sat down by the river with his brushes and easel, or on the village green painting watercolour pictures of the houses and church.

'My name is Clive Moon,' he said, sounding most apologetic. 'I'm sorry, the surgery seems to be closed but I wondered if I might see my dog? He was knocked down by a car when my nephew was taking him for a walk.'

'Oh, yes, please come in. I'll take you through to the recovery room,' said Mandy. 'I'm afraid the surgery doesn't open until six, except for emergencies.' She waved goodbye to James then took Mr Moon through. Simon was there, checking up on Sheba.

Mr Moon put out his hand. 'How do you do, young man. Is my dog going to be all right?' he asked Simon anxiously. He bent to caress the sleeping dog.

'Yes, she's going to be fine,' Simon reassured him. 'She'll be stiff for a while, of course. And she'll have to get used to walking on three legs while she's in plaster but it's amazing how adaptable dogs can be.'

'Is Mark OK?' Mandy asked. 'He was really upset.'

Mr Moon looked up at her then got to his feet. 'Yes, he's recovered now. I know it wasn't his fault. People drive far too fast through this village. One day someone's going to get killed. Were you the young lady who ran for the vet?'

Mandy nodded, feeling a little shy. 'He's my dad.'

'Yes, so I gather.' Mr Moon put out his hand for her to shake. 'I wanted to thank you. Mark said if it hadn't been for you, Sheba might have perished.'

Mandy almost giggled. Mr Moon made Sheba sound like an old balloon. But instead she blushed and couldn't think of anything to say.

'She's brilliant with animals,' said Simon.

'Yes.' Mr Moon gazed at Mandy. He had piercing eyes that seemed to look right through her. 'I can see that. You will make a good vet yourself one day, young lady.'

'That's what I want to be,' Mandy said, losing her shyness. Mr Moon was very friendly in a funny, old-fashioned kind of way.

'Well, I wish you good luck,' said Mr Moon. He took another look at Sheba, then Mandy saw him out.

'Dad will let you know when it's OK for her to go home,' she said.

'Goodbye, young lady,' he said. 'I look forward to seeing you again.' His funny, formal way of speaking made Mandy smile.

Mr Moon strode off down the path. He stopped by the gate to smell one of the blossoms on the rhododendron by the gate. He examined it closely then went off muttering to himself.

Mandy went back to Animal Ark to do her chores before tea. What an exciting day it had been. She swept the floor and tidied up – putting empty polythene wrappers into the bin, filling up the disposable towel holder. She sprayed disinfectant on all the surfaces and wiped them dry.

Going outside to feed her rabbits, Mandy thought again about Mark Boston. She wished she had asked his uncle where she might have seen him before. It had been puzzling her all afternoon. Maybe in the morning she would remember.

But when Mandy awoke the next day she *still* couldn't think where she'd seen Mark before. She lay in bed, staring at the animal posters on the wall. Then she suddenly remembered all the work that had to be done to organise the show. She leapt out of bed, had a quick shower and dressed in her usual jeans, trainers and sweat-shirt.

She had just finished breakfast when Mr Hope came in to ask Mandy if she'd like to help him take Sheba home. 'Then I've just got time to take you to the sanctuary to see your owl before I do my rounds,' he said.

'Thanks, Dad!' Mandy ran the tap hastily over her empty cereal bowl and left it to drain. She dashed out after him.

In the recovery room, Sheba stood on three wobbly legs drinking a bowl of milk. She wagged her tail when Mandy appeared. Mandy felt relieved to see the dog looking better. Nevertheless, her heart still skipped with pity. No matter how hard she tried she could never get used to seeing animals in pain.

She bent down to stroke the dog's head. Sheba whined then gave her a milky lick on the cheek.

'I've given her a pain-killer,' Mr Hope said. 'And I'll call and see her later to check her over.'

'Can she walk?' Mandy asked.

Mr Hope shook his head. 'She'd probably try, she's a very brave animal. But we'd better carry her to the car, she's still fairly groggy.'

Between them, Mandy and her dad carried the huge dog carefully out to the car. Mr Hope had already laid a blanket in the back.

They settled Sheba down and Mandy climbed in with her.

'Good girl,' she murmured comfortingly. 'You'll soon be home.'

Mandy stroked Sheba gently and whispered soft words of reassurance as Mr Hope drove slowly along the street and up one of the narrow alleyways that led to Mr Moon's house. It was called Moon Cottage and was one of a terrace of three stone houses with black tiled roofs and small, mullioned windows. There was a painting of a half moon below the crescent-shaped door knocker.

Mr Moon was looking anxiously out of the window. He disappeared as the car drew up outside, then the front door opened and he came out and ran to the gate.

Mandy climbed out of the back as Mr Hope came to lift Sheba out.

The dog's tail wagged joyfully and she licked his face all over as Mr Moon bent to stroke her. Mandy swallowed back tears. It was always great to see animals reunited with their owners.

Mr Moon helped Mr Hope carry the dog indoors.

'Put her on the sofa,' he said, shouting above the sound of loud pop music from a radio playing upstairs.

They settled Sheba down on the red rug that

covered the sofa. Mr Moon closed a door so they could hear themselves speak.

'She still looks a bit dazed,' he said anxiously. He sat down next to Sheba and stroked her ears.

'Yes,' said Mr Hope. 'She'll be groggy for a while.' He handed Mr Moon a bottle of tablets. 'Give her one of these three times a day,' he said. 'They'll control her pain. I'll pop in again later to see how she's doing.'

'Thank you so much,' said Mr Moon. 'I'm very grateful for what you have done.'

Mandy looked round the room. The walls were covered with Mr Moon's watercolours. There was one of Stony Bridge and another of Monkton Spinney knee-deep in bluebells like a wonderful, azure carpet. It was so lifelike Mandy could almost smell their perfume.

'Do you like my pictures?' Mr Moon asked when he saw Mandy gazing at them.

'Yes, they're lovely,' Mandy said enthusiastically. 'My friend James is good at art. I'm hopeless.'

'Well, you have other talents,' Mr Moon said, his eyes twinkling at her. 'We all have different things we can do well. Perhaps you would like to see my studio?'

'I'd love to,' said Mandy.

'If you want to see that owl of yours I'm afraid we'll have to get going,' Mr Hope said, looking at his watch.

Mandy shrugged. 'Sorry, Mr Moon. I'll come back another time if that's OK.'

'Any time you're passing,' Mr Moon assured her. He saw them out.

Halfway along the village street Mandy let out an exclamation of dismay.

'What's up?' her father asked.

'I meant to ask Mr Moon about Mark,' she said.

'What about Mark?'

'Well, I know I've seen him somewhere before and I can't think where. I thought maybe his uncle might know.'

'You'll have to ask him next time you see him,' Mr Hope said.

It was a lovely, warm, spring day as they drove the few miles to the sanctuary. When they got there, Mr Hope stopped by the gate and hooted the car horn. Betty came running out.

'We've come to see the owl,' Mandy explained as Betty unlocked the gate to let them through.

'He's still in the office,' said Betty, nodding to Mr Hope. 'Come on in, both of you.'

The owl was sitting on the perch in his hospital

cage. Mandy approached cautiously. She didn't want to frighten him. His plumage looked less ruffled than before. His broad, speckled wings were folded against his tiny body. His large feet were spread out to give him balance on the narrow perch. He looked so sweet and funny, Mandy couldn't help smiling.

'He looks better,' Mandy said, turning to the others with shining eyes.

'Yes,' said Betty. 'I've managed to persuade him to eat some earthworms and he's perked up a bit. I'm going to put him into a flight cage later.'

'What's that?' Mandy asked.

'It's a much bigger pen, out of doors,' Betty explained. 'The kind he'll be in over at the rehabilitation centre. It'll give him a chance to get used to being out in the open. So far his only experience of the outside world is his fall from the tree!'

'Poor little thing,' Mandy said softly.

'He needs room to stretch,' said Mr Hope. 'And try to use those wings of his.'

'That's right,' said Betty. 'If he doesn't he'll become very weak. He needs all his strength to learn to fly.'

'How will you get him to do that?' asked Mandy.

'They'll do it over at Longmoor,' Betty said. 'I won't keep him here much longer. He's getting too used to humans and that's not good.'

Mandy's heart went out to the little creature. It was true he looked better, more perky. But he still looked lost and lonely and she felt desperately sorry for him, especially because it was her own fault the owl was there. Owls should be out in the woods and fields, flying free, not hunched up in a cage in someone's office.

She let out a sigh and turned away. 'The sooner he's free, the better,' she said.

Betty put an arm round her shoulder. 'Mandy,

don't feel so bad. If it wasn't for you, he might be dead by now.'

'That's true,' Mandy said. But she still wasn't certain she'd done the right thing.

'Tell Betty quickly about the show, then we've got to be off,' Mr Hope told her.

Betty looked overjoyed when she heard how things were going. 'Thanks, Mandy,' she said giving her a hug. 'I did wonder if you'd like me to bring my display of the work I do here. I've got photographs and information about stray dogs and cats, that kind of thing.'

'That would be super,' Mandy said. 'Then people can see what will be done with the money we raise.'

'And let me know if I can be of any help,' said Betty.

'They seem to be getting on pretty well on their own,' Mr Hope said with a twinkle in his eye. 'You know what Mandy's like once she gets started on something.'

'We're going to need lots of help on the day,' said Mandy. 'So I'll let you know, OK?'

'Fine,' said Betty. 'I'll see you both soon.' She stood by the gate as Mandy and Mr Hope drove away.

Driving through the village Mandy spied James

heading towards Animal Ark with a bundle of paper under his arm.

Mr Hope stopped the car to let Mandy out and she ran across to meet him. Mr Hope waved goodbye to his daughter and drove off.

Mandy told James about her visit to see the owl. James unrolled one of the notices to show her.

'Wow, James, it's brilliant,' exclaimed Mandy.

'My dad helped,' said James. 'Then he went to his office to make all these photocopies.'

Mandy was so pleased she felt like giving James a hug. Then she thought better of it. She didn't want to embarrass him. James always blushed

Save Our Sanctuary!
WELFORD ANIMAL SANCTUARY
DESPERATELY NEEDS YOUR HELP
COME TO THE
GRAND NOVELTY VILLAGE PET SHOW
TO BE HELD IN
THE VICARAGE GARDEN ON SATURDAY
by kind permission of the Reverend Hadcroft
CLASSES FOR ALL PETS, BIG AND SMALL
THE FUN BEGINS AT 2PM

furiously whenever anyone gave him a hug.

'Come on,' she said instead. 'Let's take them round the village.'

'What? You mean put one in everyone's door?' James said looking dubious. 'It'll take ages and we've got lots of other things to do.'

Mandy looked crestfallen. 'Well, who else is going to do it?'

James looked thoughtful. 'I don't know.'

Across the road, Clare McKay, the doctor's daughter, was coming out of the post office. She waved to Mandy and James and came across to talk to them.

'Hi,' she said brightly. She held up her weekly animal magazine. 'I've just been to pick this up. The paper-boy forgot to deliver it this morning.'

Clare had been shy and hardly talked to anyone when she first moved to the house next door to James. But she adored animals and James and Mandy soon made friends with her. Together, they had managed to set up a refuge for a family of hedgehogs Clare had found living in her garden.

'What are you two up to?' The little girl stared at the bundle of notices under James's arm.

Mandy told her and unrolled one so she could have a look.

'Wow, that sounds brilliant!' Clare said excitedly. 'May I bring Guy and Sooty?' Guy was a blind hedgehog Clare looked after and Sooty was Clare's pretty pet rabbit.

'Of course,' said Mandy. 'And tell all your friends about it. We want as many people as possible, and animals of course. We need to raise five hundred pounds at least.'

Clare's eyes widened. 'Five hundred pounds!'

'Yep,' said James. 'So we need all the entries we can get. It doesn't matter what it is – pig or parrot, we'll have a competition for it.'

Clare giggled and skipped away. 'I'll tell Mum and Dad,' she called. 'They've got loads of friends with pets. They can all come.'

When Clare had gone, Mandy looked thoughtful. They still hadn't solved the problem of getting the notices out. Then, suddenly, she had a brainwave. She pulled at James's sleeve. 'Come on, I've just had the most brilliant idea!'

Before James had time to ask what it was, Mandy dragged him rapidly off in the direction of the post office.

Seven

The post office doorbell clanged loudly as Mandy and James hurtled through the door.

'Yes, my dears,' said Mrs McFarlane, the postmistress, as they dashed in. As well as being the village post office, the shop sold all kinds of things like groceries and milk and birthday cards, needles and cotton. In fact, if you couldn't see what you wanted on the shelves either Mr or Mrs McFarlane would go out the back, rummage around, and likely as not come up with what you wanted.

Mandy thought the shop was a bit like Aladdin's cave – full of hidden treasures. Best of all, there were jars full of old-fashioned sweets like mint humbugs, butterscotch, aniseed balls and delicious tangy sherbet lemons. The shop also supplied daily papers and that was what had given Mandy her brilliant idea.

'What can I do for you this fine and sunny day?' Mrs McFarlane was saying. 'A quarter of sherbet lemons, is it?'

Mrs McFarlane always had a smile for Mandy. She and her husband had known her since she was a toddler and were very fond of her. Mrs McFarlane wore her greying hair drawn back in a bun and always had on a blue gingham overall. In fact, Mandy often wondered if she had any other clothes at all. She had spied Mrs McFarlane in Walton market once and she *still* had that blue overall on!

'No, no sweets today, thanks, Mrs McFarlane,' Mandy said hastily. 'We want to ask you a favour, don't we, James?'

'Er . . . yes,' said James although Mandy hadn't yet told him what her idea was.

Mandy took one of the notices and unrolled it for Mrs McFarlane to see.

' . . . and you see,' she said after explaining about the show, 'I wondered if you would pop one of these into everyone's paper.'

At first Mrs McFarlane looked a bit dubious but then she brightened up. 'A pet show, eh? That sounds fun. Well, Mandy, I'd say yes straight away but Mr McFarlane's gone up to Scotland to visit our daughter. I'm on my own in the shop this week.'

'Oh,' said Mandy, feeling disappointed. 'Does that mean you won't be able to?'

'Not really,' Mrs McFarlane said. 'But you'd have to come and put them inside the papers yourself. I have to mark them all up you see, with people's names and addresses so the paper-boys and girls know where to deliver them. That takes a long time.'

Mandy turned to James. 'We can come and put them in ourselves, can't we, James?'

'No problem,' said James.

'The only snag is . . .' Mrs McFarlane hesitated.

'What?' said Mandy. 'We'll come and do it, honestly we will. It doesn't matter how early in the morning.'

'Five o'clock?' said Mrs McFarlane.

'Oh, you mean the day before,' James said innocently.

Mandy nudged him. 'No, silly. Mrs McFarlane

means five o'clock in the morning. Don't you, Mrs McFarlane?'

Mrs McFarlane smiled at James. 'Mandy's right, I'm afraid, James. The papers come at five and they have to be all marked up and ready for the boys and girls at six.'

James gulped. 'Oh,' he said in a funny voice. 'Five o'clock in the morning. Er . . . yes, that's fine, Mrs McFarlane.'

'Yes,' said Mandy. 'Absolutely fine.' She sounded confident but deep down she was not quite sure how she was going to get up that early herself. But it was no good worrying. There was a job to be done and they'd better do it.

Mrs McFarlane held out her hand. 'You leave those with me then and I'll see you in the morning.'

James gave Mrs McFarlane the notices.

'We'll keep one to give to Gran,' Mandy said, pulling one from the bundle. 'She belongs to a club in Walton and I'm sure she'll put it up on the notice-board.' She dragged James towards the door before he changed his mind about turning up so early in the morning. 'Thanks.'

Outside James looked a bit upset. 'How am I ever going to get up at *that* time of the morning?'

'Set your alarm, silly.'

James raised his eyebrows. 'I know *that*, but what's my mum going to say?'

'She won't mind. She knows it's for a good cause.'

'I hope you're right,' James muttered.

'Of course I'm right,' Mandy insisted. 'Now we've got to ask Jean about that tent!'

Back at Animal Ark, Jean Knox was studying the appointments book. She looked up as Mandy and James burst through the door.

'Simon said you know the lady who runs the scouts,' Mandy said. 'Could you ask her if we could borrow their marquee for the pet show, please?'

'Pet show?' Jean frowned. 'What pet show?' She took off her glasses and let them dangle on the chain round her neck.

'We're having a pet show to raise funds for Betty's sanctuary,' Mandy explained patiently. 'And we need a tent in case it rains. Please could you ask Mrs Browne for us?'

Jean raised her eyebrows. 'A pet show?'

Mandy was beginning to feel impatient. 'Jean, will you ask Mrs Browne for us or not?'

'Just as soon as I've got a minute,' Jean said.

'And if you two promise to keep out from under my feet today, I might even persuade her to let you have it for free.' There was a twinkle in her eye.

'Oh, thanks, Jean!' Mandy's eyes shone. Everyone was being so kind. Mr Hadcroft, Mrs McFarlane and now Jean Knox. Mandy had a feeling the Grand Novelty Village Pet Show was going to be a terrific success!

'Prizes next,' said James, studying the list when they got back outside.

Mandy's face fell. 'Oh, yes. Prizes. Come on, let's see who we can ask.'

The village street looked sleepy in the morning sunshine. One or two people were heading towards the post office but Mandy didn't know them well enough to ask them to donate prizes.

They sauntered along by the village green hoping someone they knew might suddenly appear.

'It does seem a bit of a cheek,' James remarked.

'What does?'

'Well, just asking people to give prizes. Maybe it isn't a good idea after all.'

'What shall we do then?' Mandy said dejectedly.

But James had no ideas either. He ran his hand

through his hair. 'I honestly don't know,' he said, looking down-hearted.

But Mandy refused to be beaten. 'Let's take Gran her notice,' she said. 'She might have some suggestions.'

James hurried to keep up with her.

Across the green they could see a familiar figure heading towards the Fox and Goose. It was Mark Boston. They swerved across the green and ran to greet him.

'Hi, you two,' he said, grinning broadly. 'Thanks for bringing Sheba back with your dad this morning, Mandy. Sorry I missed you.'

'Is she OK?' Mandy asked anxiously.

'A bit groggy but she had a little walk round the garden. Or should I say a *limp* round the garden. Thanks again for your help yesterday, Mandy.'

Mandy was just about to ask him why he looked familiar when someone called him from inside the pub. He waved his hand. 'See you two later,' he called, disappearing inside.

Mandy bit her lip. It really was bugging her. Next time she saw Mark she really would find out.

'Come on, James,' she said. 'Let's find Gran.'

They made their way over to Lilac Cottage. The sweet smell of the lilac tree wafted towards them as they went up the front path.

Indoors, Gran was sitting at the kitchen table surrounded by guide-books and maps.

'Where's Grandad?' Mandy asked when she'd given her grandmother a quick hug and kiss.

'Out on his bike somewhere,' Gran said. 'He muttered something about cycling into Walton to get some greenfly spray. His bedding plants are being eaten alive.'

Mandy sat down beside her grandmother and peered over her shoulder. 'What are you doing, Gran?'

'Planning our holiday,' said her grandmother.

'Oh, Gran, you're not going away?' Mandy said in a horrified voice. 'Not before the show!'

Her grandmother patted Mandy's hand reassuringly. 'Not until the summer, darling. We're doing a tour of Scotland in the camper and I'm just planning the route.'

'But Gran, that's ages yet.'

'Nonsense,' said Gran. 'It'll come round in no time and I like to be organised, you know that.'

Mandy grinned. That was typical of her gran. She'd been known to organise her spring-cleaning before Christmas had even come and gone. 'Oh, Gran, I'm pleased you're not going away, yet. We need some more help with planning the show.'

Gran closed her notebook and gathered up the books and maps. 'As a matter of fact, I've been having some thoughts on that too. I've decided I'll run a cake stall.'

'What a brilliant idea!' James exclaimed. Gran's delicious cakes were sure to raise a lot of money.

'And your grandad's decided to dig out that old bran-tub out of the loft and we'll have a lucky dip. Think that's a good idea?'

'Gran, it's brilliant! What would we do without you?' Mandy gave her another hug.

'I've no idea.' Gran winked at James over the top of Mandy's shoulder.

James unrolled his notice. 'Could you put this up in your club in Walton?' he asked. 'Mandy said you probably would.'

Gran admired James's handiwork. 'Did you do it, James?'

'Well,' James went red, 'my dad helped a bit.'

'It's excellent. Yes, of course I'll put it up at our club. 'We've got a meeting tomorrow. I'll take it along with me.'

'Thanks,' said James.

'And we wanted to ask you about prizes.' Mandy said. 'Any idea where we could get some?'

'I could make a special cake,' Gran suggested.

'That's a good idea, Gran,' said Mandy. 'But you'll be so busy baking cakes for the stall you might not have the time. We've only got until Saturday.'

'That's true,' said her grandmother. 'If I come up with any bright ideas, I'll let you know. Meanwhile you could ask in the village shops. They might like to donate something.'

'Now that *is* a good idea,' Mandy got up from the table. 'I knew I could rely on you, Gran.'

They left Mandy's grandmother to finish planning the trip to Scotland and wandered along the street. At the end of the path that led to the cottages behind the Fox and Goose they saw Grandad's friend, Walter Pickard, sitting in his front garden. One of his cats, Missie, lay asleep on his knees. The other two, Scraps and Tom, were curled up beside his chair.

'Hey, let's go and tell Walter about the show and ask him if he'll donate a prize.'

They ran up the path and told him their news.

'That sounds like fun,' Walter said. 'I might even enter my three beauties.' He stroked the ginger cat purring on his knee. Mr Pickard adored his three cats.

'Trouble is,' Mandy said with a frown, 'we need

some prizes. I don't suppose you can think of anything, can you, Mr Pickard?'

Walter stroked his chin with his broad, callused fingers. You needed broad, strong hands to pull on the bell-ropes. 'Young miss, you could have a bunch of my champion roses,' he said, tipping his old cap to the back of his head.

Mandy could smell their sweet scent wafting up from the rose bed beside the cottage.

'Oh, thanks,' said Mandy. 'That would be lovely, Mr Pickard.' Walter Pickard's beautiful cabbage roses would make a great prize for a grown-up, but Mandy couldn't see a youngster being very pleased with them. But she wouldn't have hurt Mr Pickard's feelings for the world.

Walter sucked thoughtfully on his pipe. Then he took it out of his mouth and popped it, still smouldering, into the top pocket of his old gardening jacket. 'And I *might* be able to come up with something else,' he added mysteriously. 'Just leave it to me. I'll see what I can do.'

Mandy gave a sigh of relief. Walter wouldn't let them down. It looked as if everything was falling into place at last.

They said goodbye to Mr Pickard and wandered back towards Animal Ark.

Coming the other way was Ernie Bell. Ernie was a gruff old man but he loved animals and that made him all right in Mandy's book. He was the only person she and James knew who had a pet squirrel. He kept him in a huge run that he had built in his back garden. Mandy and James often took Sammy titbits and loved watching the little creature's acrobatics. They *had* to tell Mr Bell about the show. Sammy would make a perfect entrant for the most unusual pet category.

'I hope he's in a good mood,' said James as they hurried across the road to meet him.

'So do I.' Mandy pulled a face. Mr Bell could sometimes be very grumpy although Mandy knew that under that harsh exterior there was a gentle heart.

'Hi, Mr Bell,' Mandy called cheerily as they ran over. She had learned long ago that the best way to deal with Ernie Bell was to give him her brightest smile and ask about Sammy the squirrel and Tiddles, his cat.

Ernie peered at them from under bushy eyebrows.

'How's Tiddles?' Mandy said, ' . . . and Sammy? I haven't seen either of them for ages.'

'They're fine,' said Ernie, looking from one to the other.

'Have you heard we're having a pet show to raise money for the animal sanctuary,' said Mandy.

Mr Bell frowned. 'A pet show? What kind of a pet show? Not like that Crufts affair where people dress up their animals like dog's dinners.'

Mandy giggled. 'No, not at all. This is for all kinds of pets, not just dogs.'

'Sounds like a lot of nonsense to me,' said Ernie. 'Why can't you just go round knocking on doors and asking for money? Plenty of other people do.'

'Because we want people to have fun too,' Mandy explained. Ernie Bell was always grumbling about something – the weather, the cost of living – but he didn't really mean any of it.

'Hrrumph,' said Ernie. 'What exactly does Betty Hilder need the money for anyway?'

'Mostly repairs to the buildings,' Mandy said. 'Some of them are almost falling down.'

'Hrrumph,' Ernie said again. 'She hasn't asked me.'

'Asked you what?' said Mandy.

'If I could repair them,' he said gruffly. Ernie Bell had been a fine carpenter in his day and still did a bit of woodwork from time to time.

'Oh!' said Mandy, taken aback. 'Would you?'

'I might,' said Mr Bell. He drew himself up to his full height. 'If she asked me I might. I'm not past doing a few repairs you know. I'm a fine carpenter. Best in the county.'

'Oh, yes, I know,' Mandy said hastily. 'I could ask Betty if you like.'

Mr Bell shook his head. 'No, thank you. I'll discuss it with her myself. When do you say this show of yours is?'

'Saturday,' said James.

'Hrrumph,' said Ernie. 'Don't you go interfering, you two!'

'No, Mr Bell,' Mandy said meekly.

When the old man had gone, Mandy jumped for joy. 'I bet it wouldn't cost five hundred pounds if Ernie Bell did it,' she said.

'He might even do it for nothing,' James said. 'Then Betty could use the extra money for animal food or something.'

A broad grin spread across Mandy's face. 'James, I've got a feeling we might be helping Betty in more ways than one. Come on, I'll race you to the butcher's shop. We can ask Mr Oliver if he'd like to donate a prize.'

She sped away across the green. James was hot on her heels.

Mr Oliver was just closing for lunch. Mandy averted her eyes from the bloodstains on his apron. She never ate meat if she could help it. But she knew lots of people did and a prize of a joint of beef might be just the job.

'I'd be glad to, Mandy,' said Mr Oliver when he heard her request. 'Betty does a grand job at that sanctuary. It would be a shame if it had to close.'

James and Mandy crossed the green towards Animal Ark. Mandy's heart was singing. It had been a great morning. All they needed now were more prizes, the marquee, a few more people to lend a hand on the day. The task of organising the show was almost done. But, of course, the most difficult thing remained. They had to find someone important to present the prizes.

Back at Animal Ark Jean Knox was shutting up shop for lunch. Mrs Hope had gone into Sheffield to the veterinary suppliers and Mr Hope was still out on his calls. Mandy helped Jean carry her shopping bag to the car.

'I telephoned Mrs Browne,' Jean told Mandy. 'You can have the marquee for nothing.'

Mandy hugged her impulsively, almost squashing

her glasses that still hung round her neck. 'Thanks, Jean. We've had a terrific morning. Everyone's been really kind. Mrs McFarlane's letting us put notices in all the papers, Walter Pickard's lining up some prizes and Ernie Bell might even repair Betty's buildings for her!'

Just then a magpie flew down, squawking, from the tree in the Hopes' front garden. Jean gave an exclamation of dismay. She flapped her hands about.

'Shoo, shoo.'

The bird gave another harsh squawk and flew off in the direction of the church. Then it circled

and came back. It landed on the roof of Animal Ark and sat looking down at them like a king in his castle.

'That's bad luck, you know,' said Jean, slamming the car boot.

'Why?' asked James.

'There's an old saying about magpies. One for sorrow, two for joy.'

Mandy pulled a face. She loved magpies with their beautiful greeny-black and white feathers and their long tails. 'I don't believe any silly old saying,' she declared. 'I think magpies are beautiful.'

Jean got into her car. 'Mark my words,' she said grimly through the open window. 'Seeing a magpie brings bad luck.'

They watched her drive away.

'Sounds like a lot of nonsense to me,' said Mandy, imitating Ernie Bell's gruff voice.

But James didn't think it at all funny. 'I hope she's wrong,' he said gloomily. 'If this show's going to get off the ground, we're going to need all the *good* luck we can get.'

'It's going to be great, James. Don't you worry about any silly old saying,' Mandy said confidently.

James brightened up. 'OK,' he said with a grin. 'I'd better go, I've got to give Blackie a bath. He rolled in something smelly this morning when I was taking him for a walk. Mum's tied him up in the garden and won't let him in until he's had a wash.'

'Trust Blackie,' Mandy said. 'Don't forget to set your alarm in the morning!' she shouted as James set off for home.

'I won't!' he called back cheerfully.

But Mandy wasn't sure if James would be quite as cheerful at five o'clock the next morning!

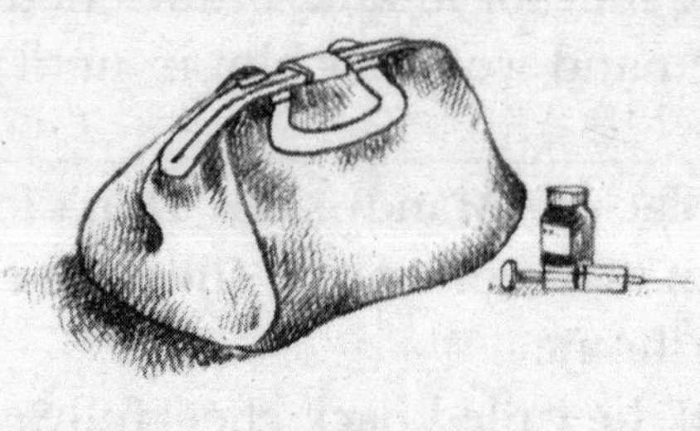

Eight

Before evening surgery, Mandy phoned Mr Hadcroft to tell him about the arrangements they'd made so far.

'It all sounds wonderful, Mandy,' said the vicar. 'Let's hope the weather's fine.'

'We've lined up a marquee,' said Mandy. 'The scouts are letting us have theirs for nothing.'

When Mandy put the phone down, Mrs Hope came through into the hallway.

'I've got to go to Twyford Farm to see a sick calf, then call into the sanctuary with some eardrops for Betty's cats. Do you fancy coming?' she asked.

'I've been there once already today,' said Mandy.

'But I'd love to go again. Betty was hoping to put the owl in a flight cage and I'd really like to see him.'

'Right,' Mrs Hope said briskly. 'Get your coat. It looks like rain.'

'What's wrong with the calf?' Mandy called, dragging her coat off the peg in the hall.

Mrs Hope was getting her bag. 'I can't be sure until we get there,' she called. 'Tom Hapwell just said it seemed very weak.'

They drove quickly through the village, over the bridge, and took the narrow road up towards Twyford Hill. Across the vale, ominous black clouds gathered. A dark curtain of rain seemed to be hanging from the sky in the distance.

Mandy peered anxiously through the windscreen. 'I hope it clears up by Saturday.'

'Jean tells me you fixed up a marquee,' said Mrs Hope.

'Yes,' said Mandy. 'But we want to set up parade rings outside if we can.' She glanced at Mrs Hope. 'It's going to be great, Mum. I'm really getting excited.'

Her mother smiled and patted Mandy's knee. 'Betty will be so pleased if you manage to raise lots of money.'

'Yes,' said Mandy.

'I've got a bit of good news for her anyway,' said Mrs Hope.

Mandy's eyebrows shot up. Betty certainly could use some good news. 'What?' she asked.

'I've found a home for the Shetland pony,' said Mrs Hope.

'That's great, Mum!' Mandy's eyes shone. 'Where?'

'One of the women in my yoga class,' her mother explained. 'I met her in the village and she wants a Shetland for her little girl.'

Mandy couldn't wait to tell Betty.

As they approached Twyford Farm, Mandy chatted on excitedly about the show, only stopping when the car bounced over the cattle grid and into the farmyard.

A young man was mucking out the barn with a tractor and loader. He stopped the engine and jumped down from the cab. He wore green overalls and a black woolly cap. It was Mike Hapwell, the farmer's son.

'Hi, Emily. Hi, Mandy. Sorry to drag you all the way up here but I'm really worried. The calf's out of one of Dad's prize milkers. He and Mum are away on holiday and I'll really be in for it if they get back to find it's died.'

'Right, let's take a look at it,' Mrs Hope said in her usual businesslike manner. She took her bag from the car and headed towards the cattle shed.

'No, it's in the house,' Mike said quickly. 'I've put it by the stove to keep warm.'

In the farmhouse kitchen, a thin, newborn calf lay in front of the stove in a huge cardboard box.

Mandy's heart did a somersault. The calf really was poorly. It was thin and shivering and looked half-dead already. Mike had covered it with a blanket and it lay with its head resting on the edge of the box.

Mandy bent down beside the calf. Its eyes were dull and lifeless. She had the horrible feeling their visit might have come too late.

'I found her in the corner of the barn,' said Mike. 'The mother had lost interest. Can you save her, Emily?'

Mrs Hope opened her bag quickly and took out a thermometer. She took the calf's temperature. By now, it was shaking violently. Mrs Hope held the thermometer up to the light.

'It's extremely high,' she said, looking grim. She glanced up at Mike. 'Don't look so worried,' she said. 'It's when the temperature's really low you have to start panicking. This means she's fighting some kind of infection. Get me a syringe please, Mandy.'

Mandy took a syringe from its sterile wrapper and handed it to her mother.

'It's probably caused by the calf not sucking her mother's milk soon enough after birth,' Mrs Hope explained. 'That means it hasn't taken in any natural defences.' She quickly gave the calf an injection in its flank. 'This is serum,' said Mrs Hope. 'It'll give her the necessary antibodies. Another one please, Mandy.'

Mandy handed her mother a second syringe. Mrs Hope gave the sick calf a second jab. 'This is antibiotic to help fight the infection. You should see some improvement by later on tonight. If not, let us know. I'll call again tomorrow.'

Mrs Hope shut her bag and stood up.

'Thanks, Emily,' said Mike.

Mrs Hope glanced at her watch. 'Come along, Mandy. No time to waste.'

Mrs Hope went outside to wash her hands under the yard tap. Mandy stayed behind, murmuring words of comfort to the sick animal. 'Please get well,' she whispered. She covered it up gently with the blanket then hurried outside.

By the time she got to the car Mrs Hope had already started the engine.

They drove along the narrow hill road to the sanctuary. The gate was closed and locked just as it had been earlier in the day. Mandy's heart gave a leap. By this time next week, she thought excitedly, it could be open again!

Betty came out to meet them and unlock the gate and they drove through.

'Hello again, Mandy. I've put the owl in that flight cage round the back. Why don't you go and see him while I talk to your mum?'

'Thanks, Betty!' Mandy ran round the back of the bungalow.

The tiny owl looked dwarfed in the huge flight cage. The cage was about three metres high and four metres long. Inside, Betty had placed some logs and a branch of a tree that had come down in a high wind during the autumn. The owl was almost hidden as its speckled brown plumage mingled with the colour of the wood. In fact, Mandy couldn't see him at all at first. It was only when he blinked his huge, black eyes that she spied him sitting on the highest branch.

'Hello, Mr Owl,' she called gently, catching her breath. It was great to see him sitting up there, almost as if he was sitting in a branch of a tree in Monkton Spinney.

On the ground below, Betty had placed two tiny dead chicks from the chicken farm.

Suddenly she heard Betty's voice behind her. 'I'm hoping he'll come down and get them when he's hungry enough,' she said. 'He'll probably hop down at first but when I get him over to Longmoor, there'll be other owls and he'll learn to fly with them.'

Mandy turned to her, eyes shining. 'He looks much better, Betty. Thank you so much. He's obviously happier now he's out of your office.'

Betty put her arm across Mandy's shoulders. 'I phoned the centre today. They're looking forward to having him.'

'When are you taking him?' Mandy asked.

'Probably early on Saturday morning.'

Mandy would have loved to have gone with Betty but there were so many things to do for the show.

'I probably won't see him again then.'

She peered into the cage. 'Bye-bye, Mr Owl.' Her voice broke with a sudden feeling of sadness. 'Good luck.'

'Don't be sad, Mandy,' Betty said. 'It'll be great to know he's being looked after by experts.'

Mandy nodded. 'Yes,' she said. She knew they were doing the right thing.

Just as they were saying goodbye, the phone rang.

Betty picked up the receiver. She began shaking her head. 'No, I'm sorry, Mike, I can't.'

The person at the other end said something else. Betty went on shaking her head. 'I'm sorry, I just haven't got the funds.'

Betty put the phone down. She turned to Mandy with tears in her eyes. 'That was P.C. Burton from Walton police station,' she said. 'Someone's brought in a dog that was turned out of a car on the motorway.'

Mandy gasped. 'Oh no! How could *anyone* do such a horrible thing?'

Betty shrugged. 'It happens a lot,' she said. 'Tiny puppies often grow into great big dogs and people get fed up with them.'

'But to turn it out on the road,' Mandy cried. 'It could have been killed!'

Betty shrugged again. 'I sometimes think that's what people intend,' she said grimly. 'Anyway, I told Mike Burton I couldn't take it in.'

'Where will it go?' asked Mandy anxiously.

Betty shrugged. 'He's going to try the RSPCA.'

Mandy stamped her foot. 'If I met those people I'd turn *them* out on the motorway,' she declared. 'See how *they* like it.'

Mrs Hope put her arm round her daughter's shoulders and gave her a hug. 'Try not to take it to heart, Mandy.'

'I can't help it,' Mandy said furiously.

'Well, Mandy,' Betty said. 'If your show's a success perhaps by next week I'll be able to take in stray dogs again.'

'Oh, I hope so,' said Mandy. 'I do hope so!'

Mandy felt angry about the abandoned dog all the way home. At a quarter to five the next morning, she didn't feel much better. She hadn't slept very well. Plans for the show were whirling round in her mind. And when she did drift off to sleep she kept dreaming about magpies and calves and Mrs Parker Smythe screaming at the sight of a mouse.

When her alarm went off Mandy jumped out of bed. She had warned her parents she would be getting up early. She dressed hurriedly. She went downstairs, grabbed a banana for breakfast, and crept out of the house.

The village looked tranquil and still in the early

morning light. The sun was just rising, turning the rooftops a deep orange. *Red sky in the morning, shepherd's warning,* thought Mandy. She hoped *that* saying wasn't any more true than the one about the magpies. The shops and houses looked beautiful and peaceful in the clear, still morning light. It was almost as if the world had stopped turning and Welford was frozen in time.

Mandy suddenly froze in her tracks. She drew in her breath, and stood still as a statue. Across the green, a large fox was rummaging about in the bin outside the post office. Its head had disappeared inside. It emerged with something that looked like a half-eaten bun in its mouth. Mandy hardly dared breathe. The fox glanced round furtively, then sat on its haunches chewing.

Mandy remembered a fox her dad had treated once up at the animal sanctuary. It had caught its leg in a snare. It would have died if it hadn't have been for Betty's sanctuary.

The fox's ears shot up as if it had heard a noise. Then, suddenly, it was gone, a red shadow disappearing up the road. It jumped a fence into someone's garden and disappeared.

Mandy saw the reason for the animal's sudden flight. James was plodding across the green, looking half asleep. His hair was tousled, his jumper on back to front. Mandy didn't like to tell him. He didn't look as if he was in a very good mood.

'Good morning,' she said brightly.

James blinked behind his glasses. 'Is it?' he grumbled.

'Cheer up,' Mandy said, falling into step beside him. 'You can go back to bed when you've done the papers.'

James grunted.

Although it was only five o'clock, the post office was already a hive of activity. Mrs McFarlane was sorting the newspapers into piles, writing house names and numbers on each one.

'Do you do this every day?' Mandy asked in disbelief. The thought of getting up at five o'clock *every* morning filled her with horror.

Mrs McFarlane went on sorting the papers. 'Yes,' she said. 'Every day except Sunday. Then the papers are later arriving.'

'What time do they come on Sundays?' James asked.

'Half past six,' Mrs McFarlane said cheerfully. 'We get a bit of a lie-in that day!'

James wrinkled his nose and ran his hand

through his hair. Getting up at half past six didn't seem to be much of a lie-in to him!

'Here.' Mrs McFarlane fished out the bundle of notices from under the counter. 'I've numbered that pile over there.'

Mandy and James began to place one notice inside each of the daily papers. By the time the paper-boys and girls turned up, the task was finished. Mrs McFarlane put a stack of papers into each of their delivery bags and they set off down the street.

James sat down on Mrs McFarlane's stool. He still looked bleary-eyed.

'There!' said Mandy. 'That didn't take long, did it? Thanks, Mrs McFarlane!'

'You're welcome,' the postmistress said. She reached up and took a box of chocolates off one of the shelves. 'I heard you need prizes for your competitions. Will this do?'

Mandy drew in her breath. 'Wow! Thanks, Mrs McFarlane. That's really kind of you.'

Mrs McFarlane went with them to the door. 'My husband will be home by Saturday so I'm going to take the afternoon off and come to your show. I'm bringing Billy. Will there be a class for him?'

Billy was Mrs McFarlane's green budgie.

'Oh, yes,' said Mandy. 'There's a prize for the most talkative budgie.'

Mrs McFarlane laughed. 'Oh, dear. I'm afraid he only says "Pretty boy". But he whistles like the kettle and imitates the sound of the doorbell!'

'Well, that will count as talking, I'm sure,' said Mandy. 'Please bring him along. We'd love to see him. Wouldn't we, James?'

But James had wandered off down the street.

Mandy hastily said goodbye to Mrs McFarlane and ran to catch him up.

'I'm going back to bed,' James mumbled.

'OK,' Mandy said with a grin. 'See you later. Don't forget there's loads of work to be done yet!'

James yawned again and went off groaning.

After breakfast, Jean Knox popped her head round the kitchen door. Mandy was washing-up.

'I saw Mrs Browne last evening. They're taking the marquee over to the vicarage on Friday,' she said.

'Thanks,' Mandy said gratefully. 'I'll go and tell the vicar.'

The surgery was full up as Mandy went through. She stopped to talk to one of the elderly Spry twins, Miss Marjorie. She was sitting huddled up in one corner with Patch, her cat, in a basket beside her.

Marjorie lived with her twin sister, Joan, at The Riddings, a large, gothic house with a long drive and wide, sweeping lawns. It had been Mandy who had persuaded them to adopt Patch when he was an unwanted kitten.

It was unusual to see Miss Marjorie at the surgery and Mandy felt a pang of concern.

'I hope Patch isn't sick.' Mandy peered into the basket.

Miss Spry's face gave a birdlike twitch. 'She's been fighting,' she said in a hushed voice as if it was something to be ashamed of. 'She's a real little spitfire, I'm afraid.'

'I'm sure Dad will soon fix her up,' Mandy reassured the old lady.

Mandy went on to tell Miss Marjorie about the show. 'Do enter Patch,' she said. 'She's such a lovely little cat. I'm sure she'd win a prize.'

Miss Marjorie looked shocked. 'Oh, no,' she muttered, shaking her head. 'Kitty might catch something from the other pets!'

Mandy couldn't help smiling. 'I'm sure she won't do that. Do come along, Miss Spry. Everyone would love to see you.'

Miss Marjorie looked surprised and pleased in spite of herself.

'Oh . . . I'll have to ask my sister.' The twins *never* did anything without consulting each other.

Mandy left Animal Ark and ran over to the vicarage. As she passed the Old School House, Eileen Davy was just coming out with a shopping basket over her arm. Mrs Davy was a violin teacher and gave lessons to children in the village and in nearby Walton. She closed the garden gate and smiled when she saw Mandy pass.

'Hello, Mandy! I got your notice in with my paper,' she said. 'How are the plans going?'

'Fine thank you, Mrs Davy,' said Mandy. 'Everything's almost fixed. We just need to organise the prizes and find someone famous to present them. Your don't know anyone famous, do you?'

Mrs Davy smiled and shook her head. 'No, I'm sorry, I don't. You need someone *really* special to draw the crowds.'

'I know,' said Mandy. 'But who?'

'Have you asked Mrs Collins? She's just about our most well-known resident.'

Mandy nodded and explained why Mrs Collins couldn't come.

'How about Amelia Ponsonby?' suggested Mrs Davy. 'She thinks of herself as a bit of a celebrity.'

Mandy pulled a face. 'Oh, Mrs Davy, we don't want to put people off!'

Mrs Davy laughed. 'No, you're right. Having Amelia present the prizes might be a bit of a problem. To be honest, Mandy, I can't think of *anyone*.'

'Never mind,' Mandy said with a sigh. 'Maybe we'll think of someone. Although we haven't got much time.'

'Well,' said Eileen, 'If I do, I'll let you know.'

'Thanks,' Mandy said. It was great to know people were so anxious to help.

'Would you like a dozen new-laid eggs from my hens to give as a prize?' Eileen asked.

Mandy's eyes were wide. 'Oh, yes please.'

'I'll bring them along on Saturday morning.'

Mandy watched Eileen bustle off down the street, her shopping basket over her arm. Mandy ran off towards the vicarage. All they needed now was for Walter Pickard to come up with some more prizes and someone to present them. Then everything would be perfect!

Nine

Mandy made her way round to the back garden of the vicarage. Mr Hadcroft was in his shed, mending a puncture in his bicycle tyre. He looked pleased to see her.

Mandy told him all about the plans for the show.

'The only thing is,' said Mandy, 'we still need someone really special to open it.'

The vicar ran his hand through his dark curls, then he shook his head. 'The bishop *might* have done it,' he said. 'But it's a bit short notice.'

Just then, James turned up with Blackie.

'Come in and have some tea and biscuits,' said Mr Hadcroft, 'and we'll work out where we're going to put the tables and things.'

In the tiny kitchen, with its old-fashioned gas cooker and scrubbed table, Mr Hadcroft's tabby cat, Jemima, was asleep on a chair by the window. She got up and stretched as they came through the door. Blackie liked cats. He went to sniff her. But Jemima wasn't very fond of Blackie! She arched her back, her fur standing on end. A low growl came from her throat. With a laugh, Mandy scooped the cat up in her arms.

'Blackie won't hurt you,' she said reassuringly. 'Shoo, Blackie,' she said to the Labrador. 'You're scaring Jemima.'

James helped Mr Hadcroft make a pot of tea while Mandy sat by the fireplace with Jemima on her lap. She stroked the cat's soft fur. Then her fingers felt something underneath, on her tummy. Mandy frowned. There was a large lump growing just below Jemima's ribcage. She felt a stab of fear and her heart turned over. Lumps could be very dangerous.

'Did you know Jemima's got a lump on her tummy?' she said to the vicar. Mandy tried not to sound too worried. She knew how much Mr Hadcroft loved his little cat.

Mr Hadcroft looked shocked. 'No, I didn't. Do

you think it's anything to worry about, Mandy?'

'I think Mum or Dad should take a look at her,' Mandy said.

'Oh, dear,' Mr Hadcroft said, his face full of concern. 'I can't take her today, I've got some people coming for confirmation classes. I don't suppose . . .'

Mandy knew what he was going to say.

'Of course I'll take her,' she said. 'Have you got a basket?'

'Yes, under the stairs. I'll get it.'

He went out and came back five minutes later with a huge, old-fashioned cat basket.

'The previous vicar left it,' he explained. 'Will it be OK?'

The basket looked big enough to carry a half-grown tiger in, let alone a cat!

'What did he keep here?' said Mandy 'A lion?'

The vicar chuckled. 'No, I think he had several cats and used to take them away on holiday with him. Can you manage it between you?'

'I'm sure we can,' said Mandy.

When they had finished their snack they went back out into the garden.

'They can put the marquee up here,' said the vicar, standing in front of the bay windows.

'. . . and tables here,' said James. 'My dad's got three wallpapering tables we can use. I've already asked him.'

'Brilliant,' Mandy said.

'And you could mark out the parade rings here,' the vicar said, indicating a broad strip of lawn. 'I've discovered some stakes and rope in the shed. They'll be just the job.'

Before long, they'd decided exactly where everything would go.

'All we need now is people and their pets,' said James.

'They'll come,' said the vicar confidently.

'Especially after that wonderful notice you sent out. How could they resist?'

Back indoors, Mandy put Jemima gently into the basket. 'I'll take good care of her,' she said to Mr Hadcroft.

'Yes, I'm sure you will,' he called confidently. But when Mandy turned to wave goodbye, Mr Hadcroft was standing at the gate with his head bowed. Mandy felt a rush of pity. A cat like Jemima was such a good companion and Mr Hadcroft would be lonely without her.

But behind her confident words, Mandy was very worried. If Jemima had had the lump for a long time, it could well be too late to treat her!

Back at Animal Ark, the magpie was sitting on the gate. It flew off as Mandy and James came up the road. It settled on a high branch in the chestnut tree and stared down at them.

Mandy waved her hand. 'Hello,' she called.

James looked at her as if she'd gone mad.

'Well,' Mandy said, shrugging. 'If by any chance he *does* mean bad luck, we'd better be nice to him, hadn't we?'

They went inside and Mandy settled Jemima carefully into one of the animal cages at the back of the surgery.

Simon was there getting ready for early afternoon patients. Mandy explained why she'd brought the vicar's cat.

'Let's hope it's nothing too serious,' he said. He went to tickle Jemima under the chin.

When Mrs Hope came in, Mandy told her what was wrong. She and James watched while her mum examined the cat thoroughly. Mandy's heart turned over as she saw the frown on her mother's face.

'It's not an abscess,' said Mrs Hope. 'It's a tumour of some kind. I'll have to remove it and send it off to the laboratory in Sheffield. They'll be able to tell me if it's serious or not. I'll ring Mr Hadcroft to ask his permission and find out if she's had any food recently. I can't operate until twelve hours after she's eaten. Put Jemima back, please, Mandy.'

Mandy picked up the cat, cradling her soft fur against her cheek. She felt close to tears. She stroked Jemima's soft coat and placed her gently in the cage. She went out to the office, where her mother was telephoning Mr Hadcroft.

'Mum,' she said bleakly when Mrs Hope put the phone down. 'It doesn't mean Jemima's going to die, does it?'

Mrs Hope gazed at her daughter. 'I'm sorry,

Mandy. I really don't know until we've got the results of the biopsy.'

Mandy felt tears come to her eyes. 'Couldn't you give her some medicine?'

Mrs Hope shook her head. 'Mandy, if Jemima has cancer we'll try to treat her, of course. But maybe, in the long run, the kindest thing would be to put her down.'

Mandy's heart sank. It seemed so cruel. Jemima was only a young cat and should have many happy years ahead of her.

'We couldn't let her suffer, now could we?' said Mrs Hope. She put her arm round Mandy's shoulders.

Mandy shook her head. Her mother was right, of course. She fought back tears for a minute. Then she squared her shoulders and sniffed. 'Sorry, Mum,' she said. 'I'm OK now.' She heaved a big sigh. 'Where's James got to? We've got work to do.'

James was in the kitchen, sitting at the table with pen and paper.

'Right,' he said. 'We'd better write out a programme of events for the show.'

They had just finished scheduling the events when Mr Hope came in.

'Oh dear, Mandy,' he said, putting the kettle on for a cup of tea. 'I'm afraid the weather forecast is pretty bad for the weekend. Rain all day Saturday.'

But Mandy refused to be down-hearted.

'We'll just have to hold the whole thing in the marquee,' she said. 'Anyway, the weather forecasters are often wrong.'

'True,' said Mr Hope. He rubbed his beard. 'Let's hope they are this time then.'

That afternoon, several people called at Animal Ark with prizes for Mandy and James.

Mr Oliver brought the joint of beef. And minutes later, the grocer arrived with a box of groceries. Then Ernie Bell turned up.

'Here!' He thrust a bundle of something into Mandy's hand when she answered the door.

'What is it?' she asked, a bit taken aback.

'Rhubarb,' said Ernie. 'That woman at the post office told me you wanted prizes. Will that do?'

'It's lovely,' Mandy gulped. 'Thank you.'

'You're welcome.' Ernie turned abruptly and strode off down the path.

'Thank you, Mr Bell,' Mandy called after him. Mandy felt very grateful but couldn't really imagine anyone being pleased with a bundle of rhubarb as a prize. Perhaps Grandad could use it for his lucky dip.

'Come on,' she called to James and Blackie. 'Let's take it over to Lilac Cottage.'

On the way, they met Mark Boston. He was taking Sheba out for her first walk since her accident. This time he had her firmly on a lead although poor Sheba, hobbling along on three legs, didn't look likely to run off anywhere.

'Hi, you two,' Mark called. 'What do you think of the old girl then?'

Mandy crouched down to stroke her. 'She still looks a bit down in the dumps.'

'She'd win the prize for the bravest dog,' James piped up.

Mark frowned. 'What do you mean?'

They explained about the show.

'Didn't you get a notice in your paper this morning?' asked Mandy.

Mark shook his head. 'We don't get a daily paper. My uncle says the news makes him feel depressed. What's it all in aid of then?'

Mandy quickly told him about Betty and the animal sanctuary.

Mark's eyes widened. 'And it's got to close, you say? Wow, that's a real shame.'

'It's more than that,' Mandy said glumly. 'It's a disaster!'

Mark shrugged his broad shoulders. 'What can I do to help? Just say the word.'

'I don't suppose you know anyone famous, do you?' Mandy asked. 'We need someone to give out the prizes – someone that'll make *everyone* want to come to the pet show.'

'Huh?' said Mark raising his eyebrows. 'Someone famous?'

'Yes,' James said enthusiastically. 'You know, a film star or something.'

'I might,' said Mark, smiling mysteriously. 'I'll let you know.'

Just then, a white mini-bus pulled up outside the vicarage. Half a dozen scouts got out and began to take out a huge canvas marquee from the back. Suddenly they stopped unloading the tent and stared across at Mandy and James. Mandy recognised a boy from her class at school and gave him a quick wave. To her surprise, he ignored her and just went on staring.

'I'll see you guys later,' said Mark setting off back in the direction of Moon Cottage. He seemed to be in an awful rush.

Mandy and James hurried along to Lilac Cottage

with their bundle of rhubarb. Mandy hoped Ernie wouldn't mind them giving it to Grandad for his lucky dip stall.

A delicious smell of baking greeted them as they went in the back door. Gran was there, up to her eyes in home-made cakes. Mandy could hear her grandfather talking to someone in the sitting-room.

'Yummy!' Mandy said, eyeing the worktop covered with sponges, biscuits and apple pies. She went to take a closer look.

'Hands off!' Gran warned, smacking her fingers. 'You can buy one with your pocket money at the show if you want to.'

Mandy laughed. 'I will – I promise.'

Blackie's nose was level with the table-top. It was quivering. He licked his chops then barked, looking up hopefully at Mandy's grandmother.

'And keep that dog away!' Gran warned again. She shooed Blackie outside.

Grandad and Walter Pickard came through from the front room. Walter had a small cardboard box under his arm.

'Ah,' he said when he saw Mandy and James. 'Just the folk I wanted to see.'

Mr Pickard handed Mandy the box. What on

earth was it? Not more rhubarb she hoped. But no, the box was too small and too heavy.

She gazed up at Walter with shining eyes. 'What is it?' she asked excitedly.

'Open it and see, young miss,' Walter said in a mysterious voice.

Mandy carefully pulled up one of the flaps. She gave a loud gasp of surprise. Inside were rosettes – red, blue, green and yellow. She looked at Walter.

'They're lovely. Thanks, Mr Pickard!'

'Look underneath,' Walter said.

Mandy peeled back the rosettes. Underneath them lay something else. Two rows of sparkling medals. They had 'Welford Pet Show' engraved on one side. Mandy picked one up and turned it over. The other side was engraved with the words 'First Prize'.

Mandy's hand flew to her mouth. She looked at Walter, her eyes wide with surprise. 'Wow, thanks Mr Pickard. They're absolutely wonderful!' she exclaimed breathlessly. 'Real medals! They're just brilliant! Look, James!'

'Glad you like them, young miss,' said Walter. 'I thought they were just the job.'

'Where on earth did you get them?' asked Mandy.

Mr Pickard explained. 'My son runs a sports shop in Sheffield. He popped them over last evening.'

Mandy put the box down and ran to give him a hug.

'Oh, thanks, Mr Pickard. You're so kind!'

'Steve was pleased to donate them,' Walter said. 'He's keen on animals too. He might even come to the show with his Great Dane. It's huge. Have you got a competition for the biggest dog?'

Mandy shook her head. 'No, we haven't, but there'll be something for him to enter. Oh, I do hope he comes. Then I can thank him for these gorgeous medals.'

'I'd better take Blackie home and feed him,' James said when he had looked at the medals and rosettes. 'I think these cakes are just about too much for him.'

'Come on, James,' said Walter Pickard. 'I'll walk back with you and you can tell me all about this show of yours.'

'Thanks again!' Mandy called as they left. She sat down at the table with a sigh.

'Everyone's being so kind,' she said. She picked up one of Gran's magazines and began idly looking through it. Suddenly, something caught her eye. She stared and stared.

'Hey, Gran, look!'

There, on the page giving details of the latest hit records, was a picture of Mark Boston! He looked very different – blond hair combed in front of his eyes, a pink leather jacket and tight jeans. But it was definitely him.

Underneath the picture the caption read, *Mark Sparke, leader of Blue Moon.*

'Of course!' Mandy exclaimed. 'His latest single's in the charts. How stupid of me not to recognise him. No wonder those scouts were staring. *They* knew who he was!'

Gran peered over her shoulder. 'Who?' she said, peering at the photograph.

'Don't you see? It's Mark, Mr Moon's nephew. I *knew* I'd seen him somewhere before! Mark Sparke's his stage name!'

She went on to tell her gran about Sheba's accident.

'Well, I never,' said Gran. 'You know, I like that band.'

'Blue Moon,' said Mandy. 'He must have taken the name from his uncle. Fancy someone as famous as that staying in our village!'

'What luck,' said Gran, wiping a smear of flour from her nose.

'He wants to come and live here–' Mandy said. She broke off. 'Oh, Gran, wouldn't it be brilliant if *he* presented the prizes at the show? I thought he looked a bit funny when I asked him if he knew anyone famous. He must have thought I was joking.'

'Well,' said Gran, matter-of-factly, 'if you want him to do it, you'd better go and ask him.'

Mandy leapt up. She would do *just* that!

Mandy ran out of the house and along the high street towards Moon Cottage. She knocked on the door and waited anxiously for it to open. If Mark agreed to come to the show it would be the last of their problems solved. Everyone would want to come and see him and the show would be a terrific success – better than they ever dreamed of. She shuffled her feet. *Hurry up, Mark,* she said to herself. *Oh, please hurry up!*

Suddenly the door opened and Mr Moon stood there in his painting smock. He held a paintbrush in one hand, a rag in the other.

He looked surprised to see her. 'Oh, Miss Hope. How nice. Have you come to see my studio?'

'Um . . . no, actually I've come to see Mark. Is he in, please?' Mandy said quickly.

Mr Moon shook his head. 'I'm so sorry, he's

just gone tearing off to Walton. He's always in such a hurry, that boy. He leaves me feeling quite exhausted.'

'Do you know when he'll be back?' Mandy asked, her heart sinking.'

'Sorry,' said Mr Moon. 'He didn't say.'

Mandy told him the reason for her visit.

Mr Moon looked doubtful. 'He's going back to London tomorrow. I'm sorry, Miss Hope.'

Mandy couldn't hide her disappointment. 'Thanks, Mr Moon.'

Mandy began to walk away, head down. She felt so disappointed, she could cry.

She heard Mr Moon calling her name.

'Please wait a moment, Miss Hope. I've got something for you.'

Mr Moon came back with something under his arm. 'Here,' he said. 'I've been hearing about your pet show. Would you like to give this as one of the prizes?'

Mr Moon thrust a picture into Mandy's hands. She looked at it and gave a whistle. 'Mr Moon! Are you sure?'

It was a painting of Sheba as a puppy. She was sitting on the patio beside a clay pot full of bright red geraniums. Mandy thought it was the best painting she had ever seen.

'Yes, yes, of course I'm sure,' said Mr Moon, scratching his scalp with the end of his paintbrush. 'I got Sheba from an animal sanctuary and I'm only too pleased to help.'

Mandy stuck out her hand for Mr Moon to shake. 'Thank you *so* much,' she gasped. 'We'll keep it for the biggest prize of all.'

'I've actually got a better idea,' said Mr Moon, stroking his beard thoughtfully. 'Why don't you raffle it? It would be a way to raise extra money.'

'What a good idea!' Mandy exclaimed. Then her face fell. 'We haven't got any raffle tickets.'

'I'm sure Mrs McFarlane will find you some,' said Mr Moon.

'Yes, I'll go and ask. Thanks again, Mr Moon.'

Mandy walked along to the post office with the painting tucked under her arm. She tried desperately not to be down-hearted about Mark. They had some great prizes now, all the posters were out, the tent was up in the vicarage garden. Everything was ready.

Mr Moon was right. Mrs McFarlane *did* have a book of raffle tickets. Mandy bought them and hurried home.

Mr and Mrs Hope were both out so Mandy

showed the painting to Jean Knox, then left it in the kitchen for her parents to see when they came in. She took the medals upstairs and put them on her window-sill. She opened the lid. She took them out one by one and laid them in a line along the window-sill. They were so shiny and beautiful, and she felt very lucky to have them. She was determined not to be upset about Mark. Everything else was going well. Still, it did seem a shame that Mark would miss the show.

Through the open window, Mandy saw her father's Land-rover draw up outside. She rushed downstairs to show him the painting.

He came through into the kitchen. 'Wow!' he said when he saw it. 'That's terrific. Where did you get it from?'

Mandy told him.

'That was kind of him. His pictures sell for a lot of money, I believe.'

By the time Mandy and Mr Hope had eaten their lunch and Mandy had done her chores in the surgery, half the afternoon had gone. There had been no word from Mark so Mandy could only think he hadn't got her message. She went back into the kitchen. Mr Moon's picture was still propped up against the fruit bowl. She decided to take it up to her room for safe-keeping.

The box of rosettes was on the window-sill. Mandy suddenly remembered the medals. She had better put those away too.

But, to Mandy's horror, the medals were nowhere to be seen. She was sure she had left them in a long, shiny row on her window-sill. Her heart lurched. Where had they gone?

She put the painting on the bed and hurriedly opened her dressing-table drawer. Maybe she had put them in there? Perhaps her mum had come in and decided to tidy up? But surely they would have heard her.

Mandy flew round the room in a panic. She opened all her drawers, her cupboards. She searched frantically in her desk. She stood in the centre of the room, her hands in her hair. What had happened to those beautiful medals? Where on earth had they gone?

Mandy ran over to the open window. She looked through on to the garden below. Had they fallen out?

She rushed downstairs. Out in the garden she searched high and low. Her dad came out to ask her what she was up to.

'The medals!' Mandy turned a stricken face

towards him. 'They've disappeared!'

They looked everywhere but they couldn't find a single medal.

'I don't understand,' Mandy wailed. 'I left them on the window-sill. I know I did!'

When Mrs Hope came in she searched as well. She took another look in Mandy's room. She peered under the bed, hunted in the cupboards. There was no sign of the medals anywhere.

'Now everything's ruined!' Mandy sobbed. 'What will Walter Pickard think of me!'

'They might turn up yet,' said Mrs Hope, trying to comfort her daughter.

But whatever had happened to the medals was a complete mystery. They had disappeared into thin air!

That night, Mandy hardly slept a wink. The wind howled round the house and rain lashed against the window panes. Mandy turned her head into the pillow with a sob. Everything seemed to be going wrong. There was no one to present the medals and now, no medals to present. Jean Knox had been right when she told Mandy about that magpie. It *had* brought bad luck after all!

Ten

It was the day of the Grand Novelty Village Pet Show. Mandy awoke early. She leapt out of bed and drew back the curtains. Her heart sank. Not only had the medals gone missing, the weather was terrible. Black clouds covered the sky and the rain was coming down in buckets.

Mandy took a deep breath. They'd just have to have the whole thing in the marquee. After all, that's what it was for!

Mandy hurriedly dressed. Everyone knew about the show now. It had to go ahead, rain or shine.

Downstairs, Mrs Hope was laying the table for breakfast.

'Come on, Mandy. You've got a busy day ahead of you.'

Mandy sat down, trying not to look miserable. She toyed with her bowl of cornflakes.

'Eat up!' Mrs Hope put a plate of eggs and toast in front of Mandy's father.

Mr Hope looked up from his paper. 'Cheer up, Mandy,' he said. 'Maybe it'll stop raining soon.'

'It's not that,' Mandy said, staring into her orange juice. 'It's those lovely medals. I wish I knew what had happened to them.'

Mrs Hope put her arm round Mandy. 'I'll have another look later,' she promised. 'Maybe they'll turn up.'

'Thanks, Mum.'

Suddenly, Mr Hope gave a low whistle. 'Hey, Mandy,' he said. 'Look at this!'

He turned the paper towards her. The headline said, *Pop star to present prizes at village pet show.*

Mandy could hardly believe her eyes. She gave a gasp and grabbed the paper from her dad's hands. She quickly read the story. ' "Pop star Mark Sparke is lending his support to a grand pet show to raise funds for the Welford Animal Sanctuary . . . " ' she read aloud. The story went on to give all the details of the show.

Mandy looked up with shining eyes. 'Wow!' she said. 'That must have been where Mark rushed off to yesterday. His uncle said he'd gone into Walton. He must have gone to the newspaper office.' She beamed a smile at her mother and father. 'Good old Mark!' Suddenly the loss of the medals didn't seem quite so tragic after all.

Mandy hurriedly gulped down her orange juice. She took a mouthful of cornflakes. 'I'm just going to thank him,' she called.

'But, Mandy, finish your–' her mother began. But Mandy was gone, rushing down the street and along the lane to Moon Cottage.

Mark answered her knock at the door.

Mandy gave him a bright grin. 'I've just seen the paper,' she panted. 'Thanks, Mark!'

Mark shrugged. 'I'm glad to help,' he said. 'Is there anything else you'd like me to do?'

Suddenly Mandy had a brainwave. 'You could take care of the raffle,' she said. 'Your uncle's given us a lovely picture of Sheba. Everyone will buy a ticket if you're selling them.' Mandy felt herself go red. Now she knew Mark was a famous pop star, she felt a bit shy.

'No problem,' said Mark. 'I'll be glad to.'

'Oh, thanks,' Mandy said breathlessly.

'What time does the fun start?' Mark called as Mandy ran down the path.

'Two o'clock,' she called. 'See you later!'

Skipping back along the road, Mandy realised it had stopped raining. The black clouds were rolling away and the sun was coming out. Her heart gave a leap. Things just might work out!

Up in the chestnut tree, the magpie flew squawking from its untidy nest. It was joined by another one and the two birds flew around in circles before settling back in the tree.

'One for sorrow, two for joy,' Mandy murmured to herself.

Mrs Platt from the bungalows was walking along with her miniature poodle, Antonia. Antonia had been one of Betty's dogs from the sanctuary.

The poodle was looking splendid in a red collar, her coat clean and fluffy. She greeted Mandy with a lick and a wag of her tail.

'Are you bringing her to the show this afternoon?' Mandy asked as Antonia jumped up to say hello.

'I certainly am,' Mrs Platt said proudly. 'I want to give my support to the sanctuary. I'd never have got Antonia if it wasn't for Betty Hilder.'

'It's going to be great fun,' said Mandy, feeling

excited. 'Mark Sparke's presenting the prizes.'

Mrs Platt looked blank. 'Mark who?'

'Mark Sparke, the pop star. Haven't you heard of him?'

Mrs Platt shook her head. 'No, sorry. But never mind, I'm sure all the young people will know who he is.' She looked up at the two magpies squawking overhead. 'Nasty, noisy things, magpies,' she said. 'They're thieves too.'

'Thieves?' said Mandy, puzzled.

'Yes, they love to take shiny things and keep them in their nests. I once heard about . . .'

Mandy frowned. Thieves? Thieves! She suddenly gave a whoop of joy. She threw her arms round Mrs Platt and gave her a hug. Of course! *That's* where the medals had gone. Mandy had left her window open and the magpies had stolen them!

Mandy sped away. 'Thanks, Mrs Platt,' she called over her shoulder.

Mandy ran indoors. 'Mum? Dad? Where are you?'

But the house was empty.

'They've both had to go out.' Jean Knox had just arrived in the surgery and was hanging up her coat. 'Sam Western's got some big emergency on his farm – they could be ages.'

Mandy's mind raced. James's dad would have a ladder. She rushed over to James's house. He was just coming out, on his way over to Animal Ark.

'They've taken the tables over to the vicarage,' he said as Mandy blurted out her story. 'But Dad's ladder is in the shed.' James dashed down the garden path and wrenched open the shed door. 'Come on, let's do it ourselves!'

Together they carried the ladder across the green. Mandy set it firmly against the tree-trunk.

'You hold it,' she told James. 'I'll climb up.'

'Don't look down,' James warned. He squinted upwards.

Carefully, Mandy climbed all the way to the top. The two magpies watched her, their eyes bright against their shiny black heads. With one hand, Mandy held on tightly to a nearby branch. She leaned across. The ladder swayed.

'Be careful,' James yelled from down below.

By now, a small crowd had gathered to watch.

Ernie Bell shook his head. 'She shouldn't be up there,' he said. 'It don't look safe to me.'

Then, as Mandy reached into the nest, her hand came into contact with something. Something round and cold. She picked it up. To her relief, it was one of the medals! She reached in again.

WORLD CL

Soon all the medals were safe in Mandy's pocket. A small cheer went up as Mandy climbed carefully back down the ladder.

James patted her on the back. 'Great, Mandy!'

'Come on,' Mandy said. 'Let's get the rosettes and take the whole lot over to the vicarage before they disappear again!'

They took the ladder back, then collected the rest of the prizes. They made their way over to the vicarage.

The garden looked clean and bright after the rain. The grass sparkled and the flowers looked shiny and fresh. Mr and Mrs Hunter had set the tables up along one side of the lawn. The vicar had already staked out the show rings.

They found Mr Hadcroft in the marquee talking to Mandy's grandmother. She was busy setting up her cake stall.

Then Mandy's grandad arrived with his lucky dip tub and a big cardboard box full of prizes. Walter Pickard was with him, carrying a huge bunch of his beautiful roses.

Soon, the whole vicarage garden was a hive of activity. People were bustling everywhere, setting up platforms, arranging prizes on a table.

Mrs Browne popped in with a megaphone. 'I

thought you might need this to announce the classes,' she told Mandy.

'Yes, thanks,' Mandy said. Her face fell. 'Who's going to do that?' she said to James.

'You can,' James grinned. 'I'm going to be busy getting the entries organised.'

Betty turned up in her old station wagon. Mandy and James helped her unload her display boards. They set them up in the marquee.

The morning flew past and soon it was one o'clock. Mandy gazed round. Everything was ready. The tables, the parade rings, posts with arrows pointing to the parade rings and stalls. On a table by the gate was a pile of entry forms for the various competitions. That was to be James's job. He would take the money and write down the names of the entrants. Her heart began to pound. Only an hour to go. She couldn't wait!

Then Mandy suddenly realised she had not seen her parents all morning. Surely they couldn't *still* be at Sam Western's?

She dashed over to Animal Ark, Simon was just locking up as she arrived.

'Simon, where are Mum and Dad? They're supposed to be at the vicarage. The show starts at two and Mum and Dad are the judges.'

'I know,' said Simon. 'I was just coming to tell you. They're still up at Upper Welford Hall with Mr Western. I've got a horrible feeling they're not going to make it!'

Mandy rushed back to the vicarage to tell everyone the bad news.

'That wretched man,' Gran said angrily. 'I bet he's done it on purpose!'

'But what can we do?' Mandy said anxiously. 'We can't have a pet show without any judges.'

'*You'll* have to do it,' said James. 'You know lots about animals.'

'I can't be the announcer as well as the judge,' Mandy said desperately.

But Grandad always looked on the bright side. 'Well,' he said matter-of-factly, 'we'll just have to hope they get back in time, that's all.'

When it was almost time for the show to begin Mandy sat down on a chair beside the marquee. Mark had arrived and was talking to Betty. Gran was standing by her cake stall waiting for her first customer and Grandad was checking his bran-tub to make sure there were enough prizes. James and Mr Hadcroft were waiting by one of the rings with Blackie. Mandy looked down at the pile of entry forms on the table beside her.

Suddenly the church clock struck two. Surely people should be here by now. Maybe no one was coming after all!

Eleven

Just as Mandy was about to give up hope of anyone coming to the Grand Novelty Village Pet Show there came the sound of a vehicle pulling up outside the vicarage. Mandy ran to the gate. A mini-bus was parked outside and people were piling out. Not only people, but pets of all kinds. There were dogs on leads, cats in baskets, budgies in cages.

Mandy's gran had come up behind her. 'Oh, wonderful!' she cried, clapping her hands. 'It's my friends from our club in Walton.' She ran down the path to greet them.

Mandy saw something else. A string of people

walking down the street and across the green towards the vicarage. She recognised lots of them: Mrs McFarlane with her budgie; Mrs Williams with her cat, Walton; Susan Price leading her pony, Prince. There was little Tommy Pickard, Walter's great-grandson, with his hamsters in a cage; Clare with her rabbit and hedgehog coming along with Lydia and Houdini, her prize goat. Behind them came Mrs Markham with Bunty. Then Mandy spied Ernie Bell with Tiddles in a basket and Sammy the squirrel leaping about in a cage.

Mandy's heart brimmed with happiness. There were so many people! She could hardly believe her eyes. To her surprise, Mrs Ponsonby drew up in her large saloon. She climbed out and went to get both Toby and Pandora from the special compartment at the back. Pandora was groomed to perfection. She had a red bow in her collar. Toby wore one the same colour. And Mrs Ponsonby wore a red hat to match. She swayed up the path in a long skirt like a ship in full sail. Even Imogen Parker Smythe turned up in her pink Lycra leggings and white fluffy sweater. Her mother held her firmly by the hand.

'Now watch out for those rats,' Mandy heard her say as they went past.

'I want a rat!' Imogen was saying.

Mandy chuckled. If there was a competition for the most spoiled child, Imogen would definitely win!

Mandy felt full of rapture. It looked as if the whole village had turned up to support her cause. This was going to be an afternoon to remember!

She greeted people as they came in the gate. 'James will give you your entry forms,' she explained, ushering them through. She glanced anxiously over towards Animal Ark. There was still no sign of her mum or dad. James was right. If her parents didn't turn up in time, she would just have to do the judging herself!

But then she saw her dad's Land-rover heading towards the vicarage. It pulled up with a screech of brakes. Mr and Mrs Hope leapt out.

'Mandy,' her mum gasped. 'Sorry we're late. Sam Western kept us talking. He knew you were having the show today. I wouldn't be surprised if he hoped we'd be forced to miss it!'

'Never mind,' Mandy grabbed their arms and dragged them up the garden path. 'You're here now. I think everyone in the whole world has turned up!'

Mandy stepped up on to the platform and grabbed the megaphone.

'The competition for the dog with the waggiest tail is just starting in Ring One,' she announced. 'Will all entrants please take their places.'

About two dozen people and their dogs filed into the parade ring. Mr Hope stood leaning his chin on his hand, watching them walk round. Mrs Ponsonby had left Imogen Parker Smythe in charge of Pandora while she proudly marched along with Toby. As she spoke to him his tail wagged like mad.

'I bet Toby wins,' Mandy said to Mark, who had come up by her side. In his hand he held an old ice-cream carton full of fifty-pence pieces. 'The raffle's going great guns,' he said.

Mandy turned with shining eyes. 'Isn't it wonderful that so many people have come?'

'And it's all thanks to you and James,' Mark said.

'And you,' said Mandy, blushing.

The parade of dogs was still going on. Mr Hope raised his hand. 'That's fine, thank you. I've made my decision.'

'Oops,' said Mark. 'I'd better do my stuff.' Mandy handed him one of the medals from her shoulder-bag. Mark strode into the ring and shook hands with the winner. Mr Hope had chosen a small boy with a Welsh collie whose tail wagged so fast it was just a blur. There was a blue rosette and a dozen of Eileen Davy's free-range eggs for the runner-up.

In the marquee, Mrs Hope was judging the most unusual pet. A row of people were lined up behind one of the wallpapering tables with cages and boxes of all varieties. There were so many to choose from – a child with a stick insect, a huge man in a leather jacket and motorbike boots with a huge, hairy tarantula, a woman with a pet hen, Ernie Bell with his squirrel, Sammy. In the end the prize went to James's friend with the pet woodlouse.

'Her name's Valerie,' the boy told Mark as he presented the winner's medal. Mark grinned and peered into the box. He confided to Mandy later that he couldn't even see poor Valerie!

Mandy was just waiting to announce the start of the rodent with the twitchiest whiskers competition when there was a shout from the marquee. Suddenly Blackie appeared with something in his mouth. After him ran Gran, waving her fist. Then came James, Blackie's collar and lead dangling uselessly from his hand.

'He's pinched a swiss roll,' James shouted, laughing.

Mandy collapsed into chuckles. She laughed louder when Gran came back, dragging Blackie by the scruff of his neck. Blackie didn't look as if he cared a bit – *and* he was licking his chops furiously. By now, Gran was laughing too. She scolded Blackie, then gave in and hugged him. 'You bad dog!' she said, her eyes shining with tears.

James had gone a bit red. 'Sorry.'

Mandy's grandmother put her arm round him. 'Never mind, James. I'll forgive him. One thing about Blackie – he's got good taste!'

Just then there was another cry from the corner of the garden. Mrs Ponsonby was standing on one of the garden seats, her long skirt held up over her knees.

'A rat!' she screamed. 'A rat, Vicar, Vicar, help me!' Poor Pandora was tucked under one arm, Toby under the other. Both dogs yelped and wriggled frantically as a sleek white rat ran round under the seat. Suddenly it shot out. Mrs Ponsonby screamed so loudly her hat fell off – right on top of the rat!

A little girl ran out from the crowd and knelt down on the grass. She carefully raised the brim of Mrs Ponsonby's hat. Two black eyes and a snuffling pink nose peeped back out at her. She

picked up the rat and held it close to her face. 'Naughty Gladys,' she said and kissed its nose. She went off to one of the show tables, still scolding her pet.

When she was sure the rat was a safe distance away, Mrs Ponsonby drew herself up to her full height and stepped regally off the seat. She put her dogs down. They both ran off after the little girl. Mrs Ponsonby bent to pick up her hat. She placed it on her head with a sniff and went off after her pets.

Then Mandy heard an argument going on behind the marquee. It was Ernie Bell and Myra Hugill. Mrs Hugill was chairman of the WI and wasn't used to being argued with.

'I tell you Tiddles is the prettiest cat in the village,' Ernie was saying angrily. 'And she's the best mouser.'

Mrs Hugill waved her umbrella at him. 'Felix caught sixteen mice last summer. I'm sure Tiddles couldn't beat that.'

'Oh, yes–' Ernie began.

But Mandy interrupted them. They sounded like two children in the school playground.

'Both your cats are adorable,' she said, taking each one by the arm. 'Now come on, please don't argue. Everyone's supposed to be having a good time.'

Mrs Hugill looked sheepish. 'Yes, sorry, Mandy.'

Ernie Bell snorted and strode off towards the marquee. 'I'm going to talk to Betty Hilder,' he said.

'He's just annoyed because Tiddles didn't win a prize,' Mrs Hugill said. Then she went a bit red. 'Felix won second place and that nice pop singer presented him with a rosette and a joint of beef.' She glanced over her shoulder. 'He gave me a kiss,' she whispered in Mandy's ear. 'He's a very nice young man.'

'Yes, he is.' Mandy couldn't help grinning. It looked as if Mark was a big hit! People had been crowding round him all afternoon. Last time Mandy tried to count how many had turned up it seemed as if not only had all the village folk come but half of Walton as well!

Mandy went to find her mother. She was talking to Mr Hadcroft.

'I phoned the lab this morning,' she said. 'There's no need to worry about that lump. Jemima's going to be fine.'

The vicar looked relieved. 'Thanks, Emily,' he said gratefully. 'I don't know what I'd have done if it was anything serious.'

Mandy was just about to say how pleased she was to hear the good news when she felt someone tug at her sleeve. It was Betty. Her eyes were shining.

'Mandy, this is the best day of my life! I've just been talking to Ernie Bell and he's offered to repair the animal pens free of charge if I provide the materials.'

Mandy smiled. 'That's great, Betty. He's a really good carpenter. Do you remember that wonderful cage he made for Lucky the fox cub?'

'Yes, I do,' Betty said. 'And what's more Mark has offered to adopt several of my animals. That means he's going to pay for their food and vet's bills.'

'Oh, Betty, that's brilliant!' Mandy's heart was brimming with joy.

Betty gave her a hug. 'Mandy, I'm so grateful to you.'

The rest of the afternoon seemed to fly past. When all the competitions were finished, Mandy and James organised a grand cavalcade of animals.

The pets and their owners paraded into the ring. Susan Price led the way with her pony, Prince. Prince's coat shone. Then came Lydia with

Houdini. Houdini was prancing about and being mischievous as usual. Clare came into the ring with Sooty the rabbit and Guy, her hedgehog, in a wooden box; Mrs Ponsonby and Pandora with Imogen Parker Smythe holding Toby's lead trotted behind.

James was next, trying desperately to keep Blackie to heel. He wasn't having much luck. Blackie kept leaping forward trying to overtake everyone and lead the way. He was determined to be first in something!

The Spry twins came next with Patch, then Walter Pickard with all three of his cats. There was Mrs Platt and Antonia followed by Gran's friends from Walton with all kinds of dogs and cats. Someone had even brought their parrot in a tall wire cage. 'Pretty Polly,' it screamed. 'I'm simply the best!' Everyone burst out laughing.

Mandy stood at the edge of the parade ring. She suddenly realised just how many of the people walking round were her friends. And their pets were her friends too. She felt proud to know them. They had all turned out to support her and James in their bid to save the sanctuary.

Mandy sighed. What a brilliant afternoon it had been!

There was a round of applause as the competitors filed from the ring.

Betty had gone to stand on the platform and was making a short speech. Mark stood beside her, looking pleased with himself. He held a bucket full of folded-up raffle tickets.

'I want to thank everyone for their kindness,' Betty said to the listening crowd.

Mr Hadcroft came up to Mandy. He looked delighted. 'Your grandad and I have just counted the money. We've raised over six hundred pounds. Isn't that wonderful?'

'Six hundred pounds!' Mandy couldn't believe her ears. She had to tell Betty right away.

Mandy stepped up on to the platform and whispered in Betty's ear. Betty's eyes widened with surprise and pleasure. 'Mandy, that's wonderful!' She turned back to the crowd. 'Mandy has just told me we've raised over six hundred pounds,' she announced. 'I just want to thank you all for your generosity. And most of all . . .' she said, beckoning to Mandy and James, ' . . . I want to thank these two young people for all their hard work on behalf of my animals.'

Mandy and James blushed as the crowd clapped and cheered.

'It just remains for Mr Hadcroft to draw the winning raffle ticket,' said Betty.

The spectators fell silent as Mr Hadcroft put his hand in the bucket and drew out a ticket. He handed it to Mark.

Mark unfolded the ticket then looked up with a grin. 'Number sixty-four,' he called. Then he looked on the back. 'Mandy Hope,' he said. He picked up his uncle's painting and handed it to her. 'Well done, Mandy!'

Mandy gasped. How on earth could she have won the painting? She hadn't even had time to buy a ticket. She was just about to say as much when she heard her mother's voice behind her. 'I bought you a ticket, Mandy,' she explained, giving her a hug. 'I'm so glad you've won – you really deserve it.'

'Hear, hear,' said Mark. To Mandy's embarrassment he bent and gave her a kiss on the cheek.

Mandy blushed. She stared at the picture then at her mother. 'Wow, Mum, thanks! I'll put it up in my room.'

Mandy took a pound coin from a tin with all the proceeds in and handed it to the vicar.

'I haven't forgotten my promise,' she said. 'This is for the church roof.'

Mr Hadcroft took it from her. 'Thank you, Mandy. If we're as successful as you've been today, we'll have a new roof in no time!'

As people began filing out Betty took Mandy to one side.

'I took the owl over to Longmoor Rehabilitation Centre early this morning, Mandy,' she said. 'I felt he had been with me long enough.'

'Oh . . .' Mandy felt a pang of sadness.

'I saw Tom Tyrrel, the man who runs the place,' said Betty. 'He said they'll keep him for three to four months, then they'll be able to release him back into the wild.'

'Where will they do that?' asked Mandy. She wanted to know where the owl would be and that he would be safe and happy and free.

'He'll be released in a place called Carter's Wood,' Betty explained. 'It's a site that they survey regularly. They know there's plenty of prey there for owls, and plenty of trees for them to shelter and nest in. Tom said there's no need to worry about him. He'll be absolutely fine.'

Mandy felt tears come to her eyes. She would love to have been there when the owl was released but she knew that the less contact owls had with humans, the better.

James came up beside her and saw her looking sad. 'What's up, Mandy?'

Mandy told him.

'Betty had to take him,' said James. 'He had to be in a proper place so they could get him ready to be released.'

'Yes, I know,' said Mandy. And although she had longed to see him just once again she knew James was right. In a few months, her owl would be free. Free to hunt over the fields and woodlands. Free to feel the air through his feathers and free to live life as nature intended. And after all, if it hadn't been for that pathetic little bundle Mandy had found on their walk in Monkton Spinney she might never have known that the sanctuary was under threat. At least now the tawny owl wouldn't be the very last creature that Betty would save.

The sun was going down as Mandy and her parents walked back across the green towards Animal Ark. The village was tranquil now. All the cars had gone and the shops were closed for the day. Outside the post office, a little black cat sat washing itself by the wall. The church clock chimed six. Mandy felt exhausted but very, very happy. She knew she would never forget the wonderful day that Welford saw its first Grand Novelty Pet Show. Would it become an annual event? After all, the sanctuary would always need funds. She sighed and linked arms with her mum and dad, matching her strides with theirs. Life was just grand!

ANIMAL ARK *by Lucy Daniels*

1	KITTENS IN THE KITCHEN	£3.99	☐
2	PONY IN THE PORCH	£3.99	☐
3	PUPPIES IN THE PANTRY	£3.99	☐
4	GOAT IN THE GARDEN	£3.99	☐
5	HEDGEHOGS IN THE HALL	£3.99	☐
6	BADGER IN THE BASEMENT	£3.99	☐
7	CUB IN THE CUPBOARD	£3.99	☐
8	PIGLET IN A PLAYPEN	£3.99	☐
9	OWL IN THE OFFICE	£3.99	☐
10	LAMB IN THE LAUNDRY	£3.99	☐
11	BUNNIES IN THE BATHROOM	£3.99	☐
12	DONKEY ON THE DOORSTEP	£3.99	☐
13	HAMSTER IN A HAMPER	£3.99	☐
14	GOOSE ON THE LOOSE	£3.99	☐
15	CALF IN THE COTTAGE	£3.99	☐
16	KOALAS IN A CRISIS	£3.99	☐
17	WOMBAT IN THE WILD	£3.99	☐
18	ROO ON THE ROCK	£3.99	☐
19	SQUIRRELS IN THE SCHOOL	£3.99	☐
20	GUINEA-PIG IN THE GARAGE	£3.99	☐
21	FAWN IN THE FOREST	£3.99	☐
22	SHETLAND IN THE SHED	£3.99	☐
23	SWAN IN THE SWIM	£3.99	☐
24	LION BY THE LAKE	£3.99	☐
25	ELEPHANTS IN THE EAST	£3.99	☐
26	MONKEYS ON THE MOUNTAIN	£3.99	☐
27	DOG AT THE DOOR	£3.99	☐
28	FOALS IN THE FIELD	£3.99	☐
29	SHEEP AT THE SHOW	£3.99	☐
30	RACOONS ON THE ROOF	£3.99	☐
31	DOLPHIN IN THE DEEP	£3.99	☐
32	BEARS IN THE BARN	£3.99	☐
33	OTTER IN THE OUTHOUSE	£3.99	☐
34	WHALE IN THE WAVES	£3.99	☐
35	HOUND AT THE HOSPITAL	£3.99	☐
36	RABBITS ON THE RUN	£3.99	☐
37	HORSE IN THE HOUSE	£3.99	☐
38	PANDA IN THE PARK	£3.99	☐
39	TIGER ON THE TRACK	£3.99	☐
40	GORILLA IN THE GLADE	£3.99	☐
41	TABBY IN THE TUB	£3.99	☐
42	CHINCHILLA UP THE CHIMNEY	£3.99	☐
43	PUPPY IN A PUDDLE	£3.99	☐
44	LEOPARD AT THE LODGE	£3.99	☐
45	GIRAFFE IN A JAM	£3.99	☐
46	HIPPO IN A HOLE	£3.99	☐
47	FOXES ON THE FARM	£3.99	☐
48	BADGERS BY THE BRIDGE	£3.99	☐
49	DEER ON THE DRIVE	£3.99	☐
50	ANIMALS IN THE ARK	£3.99	☐
	HAUNTINGS 1: DOG IN THE DUNGEON	£3.99	☐
	HAUNTINGS 2: CAT IN THE CRYPT	£3.99	☐
	HAUNTINGS 3: STALLION IN THE STORM	£3.99	☐
	HAUNTINGS 4: WOLF AT THE WINDOW	£3.99	☐
	HAUNTINGS 5: HOUND ON THE HEATH	£3.99	☐
	HAUNTINGS 6: COLT IN A CAVE	£3.99	☐
	PONIES AT THE POINT	£3.99	☐
	SEAL ON THE SHORE	£3.99	☐
	PIGS AT THE PICNIC	£3.99	☐
	SHEEPDOG IN THE SNOW	£3.99	☐
	KITTEN IN THE COLD	£3.99	☐
	FOX IN THE FROST	£3.99	☐
	HAMSTER IN THE HOLLY	£3.99	☐
	PONY IN THE POST	£3.99	☐
	PUP AT THE PALACE	£3.99	☐
	MOUSE IN THE MISTLETOE	£3.99	☐
	ANIMAL ARK FAVOURITES	£3.99	☐
	WILDLIFE WAYS	£9.99	☐